THE RUDEST ALIEN ON EARTH

JANE LESLIE CONLY

The Rudest Alien on Earth

Henry Holt and Company / New York

Henry Holt and Company, LLC
Publishers since 1866
115 West 18th Street
New York, New York 10011
www.henryholt.com

Library of Congress Cataloging-in-Publication Data
Conly, Jane Leslie.
The rudest alien on earth / Jane Leslie Conly.
p.   cm.
Summary: Having landed on a dairy farm in Vermont, an alien from
another galaxy befriends two human children and uses her ability
to change into animals to learn about Earth society.
[1. Extraterrestrial beings—Fiction.   2. Animals—Fiction.
3. Science Fiction.]   I. Title.
PZ7.C761846 Ru 2002   [Fic]—dc21   2002024094

ISBN 0-8050-6069-3
First Edition—2002
Printed in the United States of America on acid-free paper. ∞

1   3   5   7   9   10   8   6   4   2

*For those who believe they may have
alien blood in their veins;
and also for Mica*

THE RUDEST ALIEN ON EARTH

PART ONE:

"WHEN OLUU CAME..."

When Oluu came to Earth, she did not keep the form of her own body. Instead she landed invisible in the hayfield of a dairy farm in northern Vermont. Of course, she didn't know the name of the place she had come to, or what a hayfield was, or a farm; but that didn't trouble her, because she'd never been inclined to worry. She was overwhelmed by sounds, smells, and colors. She was instantly aware of life-forms: soft cylinders digging in the dirt beneath her; winged creatures in the air; huge, heavy creatures clomping over the ground in a line, heading for what looked like a place of shelter. She was eager to find a shape to contain her being; but she also remembered the advice of Old Suni, head of the Wise Ones, who had beamed her last thoughts about the mission before Oluu landed: "Wait and watch." So she flowed behind the large creatures, who cried out deep and plaintive as they walked. Were they in charge? No, she decided quickly, watching them file into the shelter and line up one by one. Their foreparts were thrust into some kind of metal brace. There was an upright two-legged one who jailed them; he was frail and colorless, clad in a loose, dull-colored garment that hid his nearly hairless form. In the alcoves above, winged beings looked down, blinking, and murmured sadly. They seemed passive. Finally, however, there entered a smaller four-legger, with a fifth appendage that swayed back and forth on the end opposite the foreparts. It was wearing a fur of several colors; it spoke in many tones, and sometimes hurled its body into the atmosphere in great leaps. *That, perhaps,* she thought; but still she watched. Later, when the jailer left, she flowed into another space, off the main one, and found something she quickly realized was invaluable: a Scripture. Oluu had functions that could translate all written language, so she read its title: *World Book Encyclopedia.* She scanned the contents and found a picture of the creature she had seen. The description said, "*Border Collie:* An unusually hard-working canine, with a high degree of loyalty and intelligence." The form seemed suitable, and, given the danger she was in with no shape at all, she decided to take it on.

Molly Harkin wished for the thousandth time that the school bus would go all the way to Four Corners, but it never did. Instead it stopped on the turnoff at Piney Road. Mr. Collier opened the door for her and Jack Molloy, grumping: "Why can't you kids be ready? Every day you get off here. Why don't you gather up your coats and lunchboxes and notebooks before we come to a stop? Why do I sit here every day, waiting for you to bump your way down the aisle and then turn around and say, 'Mr. Collier, I can't find my hat'? Do you think *I* took your hat?"

"I'm sorry," ten-year-old Molly muttered. Her plump face turned bright red. She searched frantically under the seats, until Jack shouted: "Catch me if you can!" She looked up to see him flinging her knitted hat into the air as he jumped off the bus steps and started running. She gathered the rest of her things and trudged wearily down and out. The bus door closed behind her with a hiss, as if it, too, were mad at her. She pulled her collar tight against the September chill, bowed her head, and started for home.

• • •

It had not been a good day. She had failed her math test, though the school year was just starting, and Mrs. Lockheed had asked that the papers be signed, so that all the parents would know what grades their kids had got. Her mother and father would be upset. She could imagine them now, saying, "Molly, what were you doing last night? Were you sitting in the office in the barn writing stories instead of studying?" The tears would roll down Molly's cheeks, and her parents would look sad. Her dad might pat her on the back, and her mom would make her a glass of chocolate milk. Then they'd go back to work.

The work made Molly feel guilty about her own dreaminess, because it was never done. Mr. Harkin had got the dairy farm from his own father, who had shared it with his father, too, so that it had come down through the family for over a hundred years. Back when it started up, there were children and uncles and aunts living on the farm or close by, who came for milking and haying and butchering the hogs. From the way Gramps talked when he was alive, the farm had been manageable then: hard work, but also fun. The dairy herd had grown, the milk and butter sold, the maple syrup was bought by tourists and corner stores. In summer their stock won ribbons at the county fair. Molly had read stories that sounded more like Gramps' life than her own family's: *Charlotte's Web* and *Farmer Boy.* She wondered what had happened in between.

Mom knew. She said no one wanted to do farm-work anymore; it was hard, didn't pay well, and there was no chance for promotion. Farmers couldn't provide health insurance or vacations for hired hands. Their own son—Molly's older brother, Guy—had gone to work for UPS in Burlington when he got out of high school, and he wasn't coming back. "Only rich people are buying dairy farms these days," Mom said. "They raise exotic breeds, and build swimming pools and tennis courts beside their barns. Then they hire a manager, fly back to New York, and come here for the weekends."

"Why couldn't Daddy be a manager?" Molly asked.

"Then he'd be doing the same work he is now, but he wouldn't even own the herd, or the land the farm is on. . . ." Mom sighed. "When we got married, we didn't know how hard all this would be. If we had, maybe we'd have chosen something else."

• • •

Maybe, Molly thought, as she trudged past the dirt intersection at Four Corners, then turned right down Harkin Lane. But her father seemed to belong on the farm. Sometimes she imagined that he'd been planted like a seed out in the fields, cared for by Grandma and Gramps until he was old enough to break free of the soil, walk away, and plant his own seeds. Molly understood; she loved the smell of newly turned earth, and barn animals, and fresh-cut hay. Guy was different. He'd always wanted to be in the city, rubbing shoulders with people in the crowd. Molly sighed. She wished Guy were back— he'd made time to talk with her, even when he was about to leave for basketball practice, or getting dressed for the school dance. . . .

She looked up now, shifted her backpack from one shoulder to the other. As she came over the rise, the tops of silos appeared in the distance to her right, then the roof, then the whole barn, with the house behind it, and the oak trees in the yard. She stopped to look. The bright green of the fields, the dark woods, the pale-blue sky seemed to converge on the white shapes of the house and barn, as if their presence pulled land and sky together. "This is what beautiful means, isn't it?" Molly had asked her dad once, as they stood there looking down. He'd smiled and nodded.

Most afternoons, the family dog, old Sarge, waited for Molly in the lane. When she whistled, he'd come racing up the hill. Today Molly dropped her pack and crouched to greet him. That was when she noticed the other dog.

It was also a border collie, she saw at once, and it was running behind Sarge, chasing him stride for stride up the slope. But when Sarge rushed up, tail wagging, and thrust his nose into Molly's chest, the other dog hung back. She put her hands out, called, "Good dog." It backed away, as if it wasn't used to people. Molly tried again, speaking softly. "Come here—you don't have to be afraid." She asked Sarge, "Where did you find your friend?" But Sarge only barked and wagged his tail, as if meeting Molly was the highlight of his day.

They started down the hill. The new dog lagged behind. Molly saw that it was female, without a collar. Unlike most strays, the dog was glossy and muscular. Molly's mind raced. Lately her dad had been complaining about Sarge: He was old and lazy, and ate more than he was worth. But surely Dad wouldn't replace Sarge. . . .

She ran into the kitchen. Her mom was at the table stuffing envelopes, one of her part-time jobs. She looked up and smiled. Molly was so worried that she didn't smile back. "The new dog—how come?"

"What new dog?"

"The one with Sarge. Come look."

They went to the door. Sarge was in the yard, alone.

"There was a border collie. She ran up the hill with Sarge, so I saw her close."

She and her mom checked the yard, the barnyard, and the garden. There was no sign of the strange dog.

Molly was disappointed. It would have been fun to have a new dog, as long as Sarge would be here, too.

"SOMETIMES BARNEY FOSTER CAME..."

Sometimes Barney Foster came from East Glover to help with the milking. He was retired, and restless, so it worked out well, and they gave him milk and eggs to take home. On the evenings when he couldn't come, Molly or her mother had to help; but that wasn't true tonight. As usual, Molly went to the office in the barn to do her homework; but instead she opened her journal.

The journal: she'd written in it almost every day for the past two years. It was full of secrets, stories and poems she'd made up, fantasies, gossip, but regular things, too. Now she told about the dog, the failed math test, her friend Donna's new blouse, her struggles with Jack Molloy. Would he give her hat back? Maybe, but maybe not. Jack lived on the next farm over. He and Molly had always been best

12

friends; but over the last year, things had changed. Jack hated farming and had decided instead to become the smartest boy in Vermont, so he could get a scholarship and go to college. He'd developed strange habits: He talked out loud to himself and paid no attention to what he wore or how he looked. When the kids teased him, he got upset and took his anger out on Molly. Sometimes she felt sorry for him, but other times she got so mad. . . .

Clang! The dinner bell interrupted Molly's writing. She sighed. She hadn't even started her homework. She closed her journal and headed for the house.

It was only as she stood with her hand on the doorknob, ready to go in, that she remembered. A volume of the *World Book* had been lying on the office desk. She'd hardly looked at the page the book was opened to; but now she seemed to recall images of dogs: German shepherds, poodles, hounds, and in one corner—the upper right, maybe?—a border collie, too. Who had been reading about dogs?

From the two-legged one, Oluu learned the sound for what she was: *dog.*

She had "read" it in the Scripture, using her translating mechanism, but that didn't tell her how the word was spoken. Probably she should have studied the data more carefully, but she was impatient. The change had been simple: She had pictured what she wished to become, and entered it into her objectifier. At once she found herself inside a body balanced on four limbs. She stood quietly, letting herself get used to hundreds of new sensations. Then she carefully lifted each limb, testing how the body moved against the gravity that held it down. The rear appendage operated separately; each time she tried to move it, it banged into something, as if it had a life of its own. Ouch! She needed a bigger place, one where she could practice without bumping into things or being seen.

She took slow, careful steps into the main room. The plodding creatures—*Jersey cows,* the Scripture said—stood quiet in their prison. Then one noticed her. It made a quick movement, restrained by the metal brace. Oluu passed it quietly, went out the entrance hole and back into the field.

She practiced more. She stood up on the rear limbs, then on the front ones, then tried balancing herself on the rear appendage, which didn't work. She turned in circles, jumped, walked, and ran.

She met the other dog. This came about not through planning but through what the Wise Ones might have called *carelessness.* They had often reprimanded her for being careless, and for not considering the implications of her choices. When she said "Why worry?" some of them were taken aback, and questioned her readiness for the mission. In fact, it had been unclear until the very last moment whether she would be allowed to depart with the others.

Oluu wasn't *exactly* careless this time—she simply wanted to make a noise. She'd heard the other dog say "Ruff! Ruff!" which she thought was lovely. The sound seemed to come through a gap within the forepart, inside which there were some white stones, and a tentacle. She moved her own tentacle, then pushed air through the gap. Nothing . . . She tried more air and managed to produce a squeak. That was when she turned and saw the other dog, coming toward her.

Uh-oh. What if she'd sent an unfriendly message? But the dog didn't seem upset: Its rear appendage moved from side to side, creating a nice breeze. Oluu moved her own, in response. It didn't work well when she was sitting, so she stood. The other one nudged her, made a sound. She thought he wanted her to follow him.

Oluu did. They trotted through the field, behind the shelter, and into another field, where there were cows. The other one stopped then. She waited, to see what he would do.

What he did was this: Crouch low, then take off. When he came close to a cow, he darted in and moved it away from the others. The cow shook its forepart and bellowed. The dog didn't care. He ran back to Oluu. When he got close, he leaped into the air, landed on his rear limbs, and spoke. So he

16

wanted to play! Oluu was pleased—she loved playing! Old Suni knew that. Because not all worlds contained playing, Old Suni had carefully matched her with one that did.

Now Oluu followed the other dog, but slowly, because her balance wasn't good yet. They ran in circles, then moved in and out among the cows, sometimes separating one from the group. After a time, the other dog lay down. He was quivering, and the tentacle—Oluu would later learn that this was called *tongue*—dripped a clear liquid. Oluu lay beside him, waiting to play again.

When he took off uphill, she thought that's what they were doing. She didn't notice the two-legger at the top, standing there. When she did, she saw that this one was smaller than the one she'd seen before. It held out an upper limb with five little grippers attached to it. But Oluu knew better than to get too close. Old Suni had warned her about the two-leggers.

"What are they like?" Oluu had asked.

"Not like us. They are not ruled by principle or by the standard of the common good. Instead, they're individualized. They're a creative race, but their feelings often cloud their judgments."

"Feelings?"

"You remember the sense you experience when you're functioning exactly as you should? They might call that *happiness.* And when you're impatient, questioning all that we tell you . . ."

Oluu shifted uncomfortably. She had that sense all too often.

"They might call that *unhappiness,* or *discord.* I believe they have other states as well: *joy, anger, sadness, fear* . . ."

"Even the young have these?"

"Yes, they are present from their inception."

"So they are not like me?"

"More like you than some of us." Old Suni's voice was warm. "But though at times they may seem similar they are different. We advise Earth travelers not to take their form."

"Why not?"

"Their young can be particularly heedless. Like our own, they have a lot to learn."

Was there a double message in what Old Suni had said?

• • •

Oluu surveyed the two-legger carefully. It wore garments the color of the sky, which Oluu liked, and it seemed playful, too. Soon it began to jump around and make strange noises: "Sarge, Sarge . . . good dog." Oluu wondered what they meant. She practiced them silently. The two-legger motioned in her direction, repeating the sounds: "Good dog . . . come here." Oluu didn't go. She watched it walk away. It disappeared into a shelter—not the one where the cows stayed—and closed the entrance hole behind it.

Oluu knew she'd better hide. The small one might be alerting others to her presence. She went back to the hayfield and lay down, waiting to see what would happen.

What happened was, darkness came. This was to be expected, except that the planet's sun glowed so beautifully and brightly that Oluu had to blink when she looked at it. Then a stillness came over the field, and the little winged ones sang, and breezes—almost like the breezes from her old world—crept with cooling fingers across her face. Her old friends the stars shone in the sky—different stars, to be sure, but still more familiar than anything else.

Back home they would be waiting to hear from her. Old Suni said to beam a message as soon as she arrived, and every evening after. But Oluu was so tired. Waiting one day couldn't hurt, could it? Her dog eyes closed, and her new body soaked up the last warmth of sunlight stored in the earth, and she slept.

"MOLLY DIDN'T SEE..."

Molly didn't see the stray again until the next day. Walking to Piney Road to catch the bus, she felt tired: She'd stayed up late, copying down the multiplication tables and going over them again and again. But when she closed her eyes, she still wasn't sure she could tell one from the next.

Jack was already at the bus stop. His back was to Molly, and he was muttering: "Nine plus seven, divided by one-sixth . . ." When he saw her, his thin, freckled face lit up. Then he noticed her expression. He didn't have to ask what had happened.

"You got in trouble for your math test. . . . Did you get a whipping?"

"No, the quiet treatment. Sometimes I'd rather be spanked."

"Not me." Jack flushed. Molly knew he'd had his

share of spankings—for skipping his chores or doing them wrong. Sometimes he let the calves off their ropes so that they could play; and once, driving the tractor, he'd turned under two rows of navy beans when he was supposed to be adding compost. "They taste awful," he'd whispered to Molly later. She'd laughed and shaken her head. Now he was staring at her in his owlish way, as if *she* was a problem to be solved.

"It's how you think about numbers—like they're enemies—that's messing you up," he said, after a minute or two. "They're not good or bad—they're neutral."

"Not to me—I hate them!"

"That's the problem." Jack knelt quickly on the hard-packed dirt. "Numbers are for keeping track of things," he said. "Look here." He scribbled something on the road.

"What's that?"

"It's another way of doing it—with marks. Haven't you kept score like this?"

"I don't know."

"Remember when we used to pretend we were having elections in the barn, and all the cows—even your stuffed one—would vote?"

22

"That's so long ago—we were six or seven." Molly felt vaguely embarrassed. Jack remembered the strangest things.

"But it was fun, wasn't it?"

"It was . . ." Molly thought *babyish,* but she didn't say it out loud. Jack cleared his throat, as if he knew what she was thinking and wanted to change the subject. "We had twins last night."

"Oh!" She loved new calves. "Will you keep them?"

"Only the heifer. The little bull gets sent away this week."

"I'm sorry." She didn't like the cruel side of farming; but she had grown to accept it, over the years. Jack never had. "That's why I plan to study math. Numbers can't get hurt, or feel—they just are."

That's why I don't like them, Molly thought; but now the bus was lumbering over the hill. She showed Jack. Frowning, he picked up his backpack and slung it over his shoulder. The bus rattled to a stop, and the door clanked open.

Mr. Collier was mad that it was cold. He fussed all the way to school, saying how he was moving to Florida as soon as he got his state retirement check. Molly wondered if he fussed at his wife the same as he did them. Maybe she was ready for him to move, so she could stay on the farm, work in her flower garden, and take care of her chickens and ducks in peace.

Her teacher, Mrs. Lockheed, was nice, and so were most of the other girls. Many of them lived in town: Jenny, Harriet, and Donna. Helen's dad ran a canoe store and repair shop at Spring Hill, and Amy's mom sold flower plants and shrubs from her house in Avery. They had no idea what living on a dairy farm was like. They asked Molly why she didn't have a pony to ride; and couldn't she keep one of the calves as a pet? Sara knew better. Her own folks had owned a farm until three years ago, when they had sold it to Cabot Creamery. Now they lived in a trailer near Scudder Lake and worked in town.

They slogged through the morning, waiting for recess. Then they ran outside and chose up sides for a kickball game. Since Donna was a captain, Molly was chosen early, even though she wasn't good at sports; but when the picking was nearly done, Jack was standing alone, same as he'd been the day before. His face turned as red as his hair, and he stomped off, saying, "You're a bunch of losers anyway." Later Molly tried to say something nice, but he shrugged and looked the other way.

She sighed. She had a feeling that, even though it wasn't her fault, Jack was going to get her back.

• • •

She was right. As soon as the other kids left the bus that afternoon, he moved exactly behind her, where Mr. Collier's view in the rearview mirror was blocked. Then he started pulling her hair. For a while Molly managed to ignore him. Then, finally, she couldn't. "Cut it out, Jack," she said.

"I'm not doing anything."

"I'm moving to the front," Molly said.

She did. Jack followed her. Again he sat directly behind her. Now he started singing a mean song under his breath. It was just low enough that she could hear but Mr. Collier couldn't.

"Shut up," Molly hissed.

"Mr. Collier, she told me to shut up." Mr. Collier grunted. He got mad when the kids fought.

"Whyn't you darn kids leave each other alone? There's only the two of you on this whole bus. Once I let you out, you'll be the only kids within five hundred acres, but you'll squabble then, too."

Molly felt tears rising in her eyes, but she tried to push them back. She hated being scolded, especially when she hadn't done anything wrong.

"She started it," Jack said.

"Hush up, both of you." Mr. Collier's chin was small and pointy, with gray stubble on it, and when he got agitated, he thrust it out in front of him. Molly looked the other way, tried to pretend she was someplace else. In a little while, the bus squealed and hissed. They had reached Piney Road. Mr. Collier yanked the lever, opened the front door. Molly scolded herself: Why wasn't she ever ready for this minute? Jack bounded down the steps as she gathered her things silently, then stomped off. "See you," she threw over her shoulder—she'd been taught to be polite to adults, no matter what. But Mr. Collier didn't answer. The old bus snorted and ground its gears as it drove away.

Jack was waiting in the road. He looked ashamed. But Molly was furious. "Go away!" she said.

"I'm sorry, Moll, I was just . . . playing."

"That's not how you play, Jack." They walked toward Four Corners without speaking. Then Jack called out. Molly looked where he was pointing.

Coming up the lane, running full-speed, was the new dog.

"THAT NIGHT, OLUU HAD RETURNED..."

That night, Oluu had returned to the cows' shelter to learn more about *dogs*. She learned that they came in many shapes, that the limbs they stood on were called *legs,* with *paws* on their ends; some of the foreparts were *nose, eyes, ears,* and *mouth*. Inside the mouth were *teeth* and *tongue.* The rear appendage was *tail.* Oluu read about dog activities, like *eating, sleeping, herding, working,* and *drinking water.* As soon as she read about *food,* she realized that the odd, crawling sensations coming from inside her were *hunger.* The Scripture said *"dog chow"* was an antidote, but she didn't know what it looked like, or where to get it. She decided to ask the other dog.

He was glad to see her. He moved his *tail* back and forth and pushed against her with his *nose*.

She made sounds, trying to ask about *food;* but he didn't understand. She wondered if he could read the Scripture—then she could show him. But the large shelter—called *barn*—was busy, with a pair of full-grown two-leggers, or *people,* locking up the cows. The small *human* had left early, with a *saddle* on her *back.* Oluu thought there might be more people in the shelter, and she was right: Another emerged after the small one left and set something on the ground. The dog rushed over and began what Oluu was sure must be *eating.* She watched, hidden, as he downed the food. The crawling inside her began to feel like something alive and struggling.

Later she found something that helped. After the people left the barn, she went exploring there. In a small enclosure on the lowest level, she found the resting spots of large, noisy feathered ones. They contained warm, lovely-smelling ovoids. When she fractured one with her tooth, the insides ran into her mouth. It was gooey and delicious. The feathered ones waved their wings and shrieked about something in a language she couldn't understand. She ate another ovoid, then another, until they were all gone. Maybe that was *dog chow.* She hoped so.

• • •

She read more Scripture. The feathered ones were *chickens,* subspecies *Rhode Island reds.* The ovoids they produced were not dog chow but *eggs.* They were food for other creatures besides dogs. So were the *chickens* themselves. Oluu had to run that information through her system twice before she could absorb it. Was she actually on a planet where creatures ate one another up?

She had been told that it could happen, that there were worlds where it did. The Wise Ones said there was a reason: Some planets could support only limited growth, and eating one another was a way of controlling that. Still, cannibalism repulsed her. But perhaps there were creatures that weren't. Perhaps the small human being—the one who spoke to her so nicely—was an exception.

She found the other dog lying in the sun. She wanted to ask, "Where is dog chow?" But when she considered it, she realized that she'd never heard the dog use words. That was odd, since he seemed to understand them. . . . Perhaps, Oluu thought, he wasn't the smartest of the species. Still, she liked the way he smelled, and his behavior had certainly been friendly.

They played together, like before. Afterward she saw him look toward the crest of the hill, as if he were waiting for something. Oluu trotted up the road, and he followed. When they got to the top, he lay down. Oluu put her nose to the ground and smelled the little human's trail. She followed the scent.

It wasn't long before she saw it walking toward her. Oluu remembered how nicely the small one had spoken. As before, it crouched down and beckoned for her to come. Something in her dog body liked that, and she moved her tail back and forth. "Good dog," the small one said again, and out of courtesy, Oluu returned the greeting as carefully as she could: "Good dog."

"MOLLY KNEW SHE HADN'T..."

Molly knew she hadn't heard what she thought she heard, because it was impossible. She stood with her mouth open. Finally, she said, more to herself than to the dog, "You didn't say that." She patted it on the head. "Dogs don't talk," she said kindly.

She got down and looked it in the eye. "Did you say something or not?" The dog stared back at her. Its expression seemed intelligent. Just to satisfy herself, Molly asked: "Did you say *good dog*?"

"Good dog," the dog replied.

• • •

Its voice was weird. That was the next thing Molly thought, after feeling some relief that she hadn't simply imagined the whole thing. She took a deep breath. "You can talk," she said. "How in the world did you learn?"

The dog wagged its tail.

"What else can you say?"

It stared at her.

"Do you understand me?"

Eyes, staring.

"Say *good dog* again."

It complied politely: "Good dog."

"This is *so* weird," Molly said out loud.

She was glad that Jack hadn't hung around; he'd had chores waiting at home. On the other hand, if he'd stayed, they could have figured out what to do. Now she was on her own. If she told, would they believe her? What would happen? Would the dog be taken away? Would someone try to sell it to the circus or a science lab?

There were other worries, too, because the dog had been inside a chicken coop. There was yellow gunk around its muzzle: egg. Molly wiped it away with her skirt. "You can't steal eggs," she warned the dog. "Farmers will shoot you for that." It wagged its tail, so she knew it didn't understand. She tried something easier:

"Where's Sarge?"

The dog raised its head, examined her shrewdly. It turned and trotted down the lane.

Sarge lay waiting under the pine trees on the hilltop. In a minute he was thrusting his gray muzzle into Molly's hands. She dropped her backpack, sat down, and faced the dogs. "What's going on here?" she asked sternly. "How do you two know each other? Who taught this dog to talk?"

Silence.

Molly stared at Sarge's grizzly face, at his lop ear, nicked where he'd been bitten by a rogue cow. His fur was clumped and ragged. The new dog was shiny and bright, and its teeth shone. Had it run away from someone's farm? "You'd have a collar, though," Molly answered her own question.

Then she got an idea. At first it seemed strange, but, strange as things already were, what was wrong with trying? She pointed to herself. "My name is Molly. Can you say that?"

The dog stared.

"And this is Sarge. Sarge is a dog, like you. Can you say *Sarge*?"

"Saaarge," the dog said.

Molly's heart began to pound. "And I'm Molly— Molly." She pointed to herself again. "Can you say that, too?"

"Molllleeee."

33

"You *can* talk." Molly gulped. "You can actually talk!"

The dog waited.

"Say my name again."

The dog didn't do anything. Molly pointed to herself.

"Mollllleeee," the dog said.

• • •

What she figured out was this: The dog was *learning* to talk. There was ordinary stuff it didn't know that Sarge did, because he'd heard it over and over. On the other hand, the dog seemed eager to learn and to communicate. Maybe it was some kind of genius. Whatever it was, Molly wanted to protect it.

"We'll find a hiding place," she said.

She knew exactly where to look. Years ago, when she was picking blackberries, she'd come across the stone foundation of an old house in a clearing in the woods. There was a spring nearby, with a tiny graveyard beside it. Three of the four gravestones had the names and dates of babies. The last was of the mother, who'd died giving birth. Molly used to imagine that the children had survived, and that the house stood as it had when it was built. There would have been lilacs and rosebushes, she thought, yellow curtains against the brown frame of the walls, and a stone chimney rising from the end of the house, where there was always a fire blazing and loaves of bread in the baking oven that was part of the flue. The children would have welcomed her like a sister, the sister she herself had never had. She'd pretended to pick violets for them, or braid their hair, or fetch them glasses of cold, clear water from the spring. Her game had lasted for years; in fact, she had played once this summer, feeling foolish but enjoying herself anyway. No one ever went to the clearing except her.

But there were problems. The foundation was deep enough to contain the dog—she herself used an old tree trunk to climb in and out—but there was no roof, no shelter from the rain or snow. If the dog howled, people might find it. What if it spoke to them? Molly sighed.

At last she settled on a plan: to tie the dog in the woods for the rest of the afternoon. She made it a collar from some rope. But when she tied another rope to a tree, and tried to attach that to the collar, the dog nimbly jumped aside. It grabbed her skirt in its mouth and pulled, as if it were trying to lead her somewhere. It trotted ahead, into the hayfield.

It had made a nest there. She could tell from the way the hay was bent and smoothed into an oval that was the perfect shape for the dog's body. The dog looked at her deliberately. Then it lay down.

"You want to wait here, is that it?" Molly asked softly.

The dog didn't answer.

"That's okay." Molly got down low, so they were face to face. "But there's something you have to promise: You can't eat any more eggs. We sell those eggs to the store, so we need them. And don't take them from anybody else's barn, either. Around here, dogs that steal eggs get shot."

But Molly had no way of knowing whether the dog understood.

• • •

It was there when she came looking for it after supper. They slipped into the barn by the side door and went to the office. To her surprise, the dog went right to the *D* volume of the *World Book,* sat down, and flipped the pages with its paw until it came to "Dog Breeds: Border Collie."

"Yes, that's what you are." Molly watched, astounded, as the dog's eyes scanned that page and then the next. It put its nose down on one spot.

Molly read out loud: "Border collies should be fed three cups of dog chow daily."

"Oh my gosh, I'm sorry. . . . I'll get you some. . . ." She ran off, then returned with a paper bag filled with Sarge's dog meal. She poured it into one of the cats' pans. The dog swallowed the food greedily. Then it lay down, stomach bulging. Molly started asking questions:

"Why can you speak?"

"How did you learn English?"

"Are you actually a dog?"

But the dog didn't even look at her. It closed its eyes slowly, thumped its tail twice on the barn floor, and started snoring.

• • •

Molly took out her journal. She wrote down everything that had happened since she got off the bus. After a time, the dog stopped snoring, opened one eye, looked vaguely at the notebook in front of her. It sat up, rested its nose on the desk, and seemed to scan what she'd just written. It looked at her and said, "Good dog."

"*You're* a dog—I'm a person!" Molly wrote that word in large letters in the journal, then drew a stick figure of a human. She drew a dog and wrote

37

"Dog" underneath it. "See the difference—this is you, this is me. You're a dog—"

The dog said, "Per . . . son . . . Molly."

"That's right—I'm a person, and my name is Molly. You're a dog, like Sarge, only you're not Sarge, 'cause that's *his* name. What I want to know is, what's *your* name?"

"Name . . . Molly." The dog pushed its nose into the girl's shoulder, to show it meant her. It couldn't point to itself, so it just sat up straight.

"Name . . . Oluu."

"Oluu?"

It wagged its tail and said again, "Oluu."

"OLD SUNI ISSUED A WARNING..."

Old Suni issued a warning before they left: "Tell no one." Oluu hadn't been paying as much attention as she should, because she was eager to get on with the adventure. Now she couldn't recall exactly what Old Suni meant. Was she to tell no one her name? Or was the secret that she came from another galaxy? The second was what she *thought* Old Suni had said. Whatever it was, she'd been emphatic about it: "Though they aren't always obvious, all the planets contain enemies. Do not reveal your identity. You do so only at the gravest risk."

But she hadn't revealed her identity, Oluu reassured herself that night. After all, what was a name? And the *person* had started the process, not Oluu; so, if Oluu had said a little too much, it wasn't really her fault. . . .

Molly was a good *person.* Oluu felt bad for her that she looked so horrible: those two long, silly *legs* to balance on, with *feet* sticking out the ends, and hardly any fur. Her foreparts were flat, and, like a dog, she had little hard white things in her mouth: *teeth,* the Scripture called them. On the other hand, she seemed smarter than Sarge. She could read and create Scripture; and though the ciphers she used looked different, they could be translated into Oluu's system. Her verbal communications had both specific and symbolic meanings. Oluu had been able to grasp some of them, and Molly seemed interested in teaching her more. That was good.

But not everything was good. Oluu sensed that Molly was *worried* about her presence. She had warned Oluu to stay hidden during the day. She also warned her about eggs. She had drawn a picture, labeled it, spoken the word *eggs;* and she had written beneath that picture, "Dogs must not eat eggs." She had done this three times, speaking the words clearly, so that Oluu recognized them now.

Oluu wanted to ask, why? She wanted to tell Molly that between eggs and dog chow she *preferred* eggs. Dog chow was thick and mealy, and tasted like dirt; eggs were fragrant and delicious. The outer part made a wonderful crackling sound when you broke it, and then your mouth was flooded with something warm and runny and lovely. Oluu sighed. She tried to erase eggs from her memory circuits; but they wouldn't go. Then she thought of something that made her feel better. Molly had said, "Dogs must not eat eggs." This was the plural form in their language. So perhaps Oluu could eat *one* egg. Molly hadn't said anything about that.

• • •

She'd learned other things from Molly, too: about how she lived, and the other creatures that lived nearby. The land they occupied was called a *farm.* The *farm* grew food for humans and other animals, and also produced a liquid nourishment, called *milk.* Molly said the farm was *hard work,* and didn't make enough *money.* Oluu didn't always understand. Molly talked fast, yet her writing seemed laborious and slow. Perhaps in this world, Oluu thought, persons learned oral speech before they learned to write.

Molly taught her about the socializing units. Most people had *mother* and *father* in their units, and sometimes others, closer to their age: *brother* and *sister.* A newly formed person was called *baby.* It was either *male* or *female,* for later reproduction; male babies were *boys,* and females were *girls.* A baby walked on four legs, like a dog, couldn't speak, and had to be cared for by others.

The shelter that people stayed in was called a *house.* The humans kept their food there, and their nests, which were called *beds.*

Molly said the *barn* was better. She said it smelled better (*smell* was what your *nose* was for—pale and wedge-shaped on people, round and black on dogs). But the house smelled good when her mother was preparing food. Oluu thought, *I bet the mother isn't preparing dog chow.*

Molly taught her the names of animals. There were the ones Oluu had already read about and seen in the encyclopedia: *cows* and *chickens; rabbits* and *pigs; birds* and *cats. Horses* and *ponies* were Molly's favorites. These creatures were mostly *domestic:* Some were *pets,* others worked like slaves or were cut up, cooked, and served as food for their human owners. There were also *wild* animals. *Monkeys, apes,* and *chimpanzees* were part of the two-legger family, but without the written Scriptures of human beings. Tiny creatures with high-pitched voices were called *insects.* Other species lived in the rivers and seas. Some of these, *whales* and *dolphins,* had their own speech. Another sort, called *fishes,* did not.

Oluu loved learning about the planet. She wished Molly would write faster, faster! On the other hand, as Molly spoke, Oluu began to sense the cadence and organization of people language. It was an emotional language, where meaning and feeling were closely tied.

It got late down in the barn. Oluu guessed that the sky outside was dark now, the temperatures falling. Then a human came for Molly. Its *voice* appeared first, winding from the big *door* through the *rooms.* Molly jumped up, grabbed Oluu, and pulled her behind the desk. To the strange voice, she answered: "Coming!" "You're late—it's past your bedtime." "Sorry, I'll be right up." Molly waited for a minute, listening. Then she whispered, "Go back to your nest in the field. They'll be here in the morning to milk the cows, and they mustn't see you." Oluu understood the gist of what was said:

Go . . . nest . . . milk . . . cows . . . see you. She nudged Molly with her nose and whispered, "Good dog." Molly shook her head. "Good *night,* Oluu."

"Good night," Oluu whispered, in her nest in the hayfield. She wasn't sure what it meant. She sniffed with her nose, smelling grass and earth and air. From the people-house came dark clouds of something Molly'd called *smoke.* It was fragrant, in an odd way, reminiscent of vapors on her own planet. She wondered what the ones back home were doing now. Thinking of them, her processor whirred softly, and she closed her eyes and went to sleep.

"WHEN MOLLY WOKE UP..."

When Molly woke up, the first thing she thought of was Oluu. The second thing was her homework, which wasn't done! Quickly she unzipped her backpack and pulled out her assignment book. A page of math problems, six sentences to diagram. How could she have forgotten?

She got started, her notebook balanced on her knees. The first two problems were easy, but the third stopped her cold. How did you figure 12 percent of 100? Did you divide or multiply?

She switched to grammar. "The spotted pony jumped over the hedge." *Pony* was the subject, *jumped* the verb—so far, so good. *The* and *spotted* were modifiers—they called them adjectives, didn't they? She was about to add them to the diagram when her bedroom door swung open. Her mother stared. "What in the world are you doing, Molly?"

"I'm finishing my homework."

"You mean, after all that time down in the barn, you didn't get your homework done?"

"I did—it's just—there was something I forgot." Molly hated lying. She turned red.

"Molly . . ." Her mother's voice was kind. "Were you down there daydreaming?"

It seemed like the easiest explanation. "I . . . I guess."

"Oh, honey . . ."

"I'm sorry, Mom."

"Get dressed quickly and finish up. I'll make your lunch, just this once."

• • •

She threw on sweatpants and a sweater, socks and shoes. The grammar wasn't hard, but Molly didn't work well under pressure: All the sentences seemed to run together, with their subjects, verbs, and prepositions. Not only that, but she couldn't stop thinking about the dog. She even looked in her journal, to make sure the pictures and explanations were actually there. They were.

She headed for the bus stop. When she got to Piney Road, Jack saw her coming and waved. "What happened to that dog?"

Molly didn't know what to say. "It ran away," she mumbled.

"Where to?"

"Into the woods."

Jack eyed her carefully. "It didn't, really," he said.

But Molly didn't have the energy to argue. She turned away, thinking of other things: Oluu, and the pictures in the journal, and her sloppy, incorrect homework.

"OLUU WAITED TILL THE *PEOPLE* LEFT..."

Oluu waited till the *people* left the *barn* before she went to get the *egg*. Today the entrance to the nesting room was fastened with a metal latch. Oluu examined it, figured it out, and moved it with her paw.

The chickens weren't pleased to see her. They shrieked and flapped their wings. She took her time, since she could only have one egg. She looked in each nest, sniffing to see which one smelled the best and was the largest. A chicken refused to leave her place. Oluu pushed her with her nose; the chicken shrieked. She pushed her again. The chicken did something sharp with her forepart, right on Oluu's nose! Ouch!

Oluu barked. The chickens were all shrieking now; some were flying and leaping from one side of the space to the other. Small, white, fluffy things drifted in the air. Oluu tasted one: no good. She went back to the nest, where the chicken sat on what Oluu was sure was the biggest, best-tasting egg. She barked as loud as she could. The chicken gave up then and got off. Sure enough, there was a whole collection of eggs. Oluu nosed each of them carefully, looking for the one that she would eat. She supposed, later, that the human must have crept up behind her, because right then he grabbed her by the neck. His words sounded like "Got you!"

• • •

He put a metal chain around her neck and locked her into prison, with the cows. When he left, she tried to chew the metal with her teeth. But they weren't strong enough. She lay down, wondering what was going to happen.

He came back with another human. This one's voice sounded like Molly's. But Oluu couldn't understand most of what it said, or the other one, either.

"I bet somebody couldn't keep her after she got big. Instead of advertising, they decided to go out in the country and dump her! Just threw her out of the car and kept on going, like they didn't have a care in the world."

"You don't know that."

"It's what I'm guessing. Molly saw her day before yesterday, up on the hill, but when we looked again, she'd disappeared. I'll bet she came back yesterday and got the eggs, and then came back today."

"There were feathers in her mouth."

"But no dead hens. They're all there, Louis—all twenty-three. I counted, so I know."

There was silence for a moment, a silence in which even Oluu could feel the tension.

"Louis, I'd like to try and find someone who wants a dog. Or else call the pound, to see if they have room for her."

"She'll break free and be right back at it. You know as well as I do, Kay, once they've been inside the henhouse and gotten that first taste, it's in their blood."

Oluu didn't look at the people. She knew better than to speak to them. Then the higher voice said, "At least let me bring her something. Let me bring her one good meal, if it's going to be her last."

"All right," the other one said. They made scraping noises with their feet that told Oluu they were going to leave.

"You know I don't like doing it," the same one said. "You know that, don't you, Kay?"

. . .

When they came back, the humans brought food: not dog chow but something much, much better. Oluu gulped it happily. Maybe she'd been wrong, thinking that the big ones were dangerous. She made dog sounds and moved her *tail,* so that they would know she liked them.

. . .

Her captor led her past the field. He carried tools: one with curved metal on the end; the other, straight and long. Oluu had seen a picture of that back home, but she couldn't remember what it was.

They stopped. He tied the chain around a tree so that she couldn't run away. He wiped his paws—no, Oluu thought, not paws, *hands*—on his garment.

He patted her head. "I hate to do it." Oluu liked being patted, so she moved her tail. "You had no fault, none at all." He lifted the long object, opened it up. Oluu stared. She remembered now—they'd seen that in the preparation course. There were lots of dangers in the different worlds, and of course back then she hadn't known which she was assigned to, or whether she was going at all. Still, she must recall something. . . . For Earth, the list had *bombs, poisons, cars, guns.* . . . *Guns?* Her mind backtracked. She went behind the tree, where the person couldn't see.

When the human being came to pull Oluu back into the open, he found only the chain and collar, lying on the ground.

"AS SOON AS MOLLY GOT OFF THE BUS..."

As soon as Molly got off the bus, she said good-bye to Jack and ran down the lane, looking for Oluu. Sarge was waiting in the road, alone. Molly searched for Oluu in the hayfield, in the barn, at the old foundation. There was no sign of her. By the time Molly went into the kitchen, she was nervous.

Mrs. Harkin was baking gingerbread. That was one of Molly's favorites, but today she didn't feel like eating. She looked out the window three times. Finally, she asked—trying to keep her voice casual—"That stray dog wasn't around here, was it? You know, the one I told you about. . . ."

Her mother's face changed. Molly's heart beat faster.

"Honey, that dog was stealing eggs. Yesterday we

didn't get a single one, and this morning your dad found her in the chicken coop. He took her out . . ."

Molly put her hands over her ears.

"Wait!" Her mom was calm, deliberate. "The dog got *away*. It ducked behind a tree and managed to slip the chain. By the time Louis got close, it had disappeared into the woods."

"Oh . . . oh . . ." Molly just sat there, trying to stay calm. She didn't know whether to laugh or cry.

"OLUU PUFFED OUT..."

Oluu puffed out her streaked brown feathers. She was indignant. Why hadn't anyone warned her this planet was so dangerous? Though she did recall one of the Wise Ones lecturing the class:

"On Earth the living compete with one another for nourishment and shelter. Only the fit and the lucky survive. Some of their tools are pictured here."

But hadn't Oluu been busy getting ready? She had glanced at the list, certainly—that's why she remembered *gun*—but it was a long, long list, and there had been so much to do before she left.

• • •

Oluu couldn't stay angry long. She thought of the person's face when he saw the empty chain. He'd walked all around the tree, staring. Afterward he

55

kept scratching his head, looking into the woods, and calling, "Come back!"

But the dog was gone. There had been only seconds to make a choice. As she struggled with the chain, she'd glimpsed a small *bird* in the branches of the tree above. It was looking down and moving its wings as if to say, *Hurry, hurry!* She'd used her powers quickly. Then, to the *bird's* astonishment, there were two *birds. . . .*

Oluu liked being a *bird.* The tree smelled lovely, and the breeze ruffled her *feathers.* She stretched her wings to look at them. Each was a slightly different pattern and shape from the one beside it: some long and thin, others short and fluffy. The spot where her round, black nose had been was now a hard triangle. When she tried to bark, *churr-churr-churr* came out instead.

The bird nearby sat watching. It spoke what sounded like a warning. Others from the trees around joined in with emphatic voices. Then they jumped, spread their wings, and flew. Oluu stayed put. A bird came back, fluttering in front of her. She thought it wanted her to come. But she didn't know how to fly. Was it something birds did naturally? She tipped forward, off the branch.

She plummeted downward. The ground, which had been far below, was rushing at her. Somewhere up above, the other bird shrieked: "Spread your wings!"

Oluu did. She banked abruptly to the left, then straightened out. A few hard flaps carried her up; shifting her tail position helped her turn to either side. If she moved her wings carefully and steadily, braking with her tail, she could glide just above the tall grasses. Then she could see everything: the rough tops of the haystalks, stones, grass, tiny creatures rushing here and there as if they had a million things to do and not enough time to do them in. The hayfield—the very one where she'd been sleeping every night—was a spectacle! Here were insects with bright, colorful wings, rasping music, and now, to the left, a large ropelike object ending in a lumpy mound of plant stalks. Above her, the other bird shrieked again, but Oluu was curious. She flew closer. Almost hidden among the tops of the grasses were two pointy, furry triangles. *"Cat! Cat!"* the bird screamed. The four-legger sprang. Oluu felt the air from his mouth like a hot wind, felt the tips of something sharp raking against her sides. She fluttered free and flapped with all her might. Inside her, something was trembling so fast it felt like it might break apart. *Fear,* she thought afterward, that was the feeling they call *fear.* . . .

Later she found the other birds, perched inside a bush. When she joined them, their voices sounded scolding. She didn't like being scolded. She fluffed her feathers and tried to act as if she didn't care.

• • •

That night, she flew to the barn to learn more about birds; but the Scripture was too heavy for her to move. She needed help! She went to Molly's *window,* tapped it with her nose. Molly was asleep. Oluu tapped harder. Finally, Molly's face appeared on the other side.

"What's out there?"

"Oluu." Her voice was chattery and low.

"What was that? Oh, it's a little bird. . . ." Molly opened the window just a bit. She seemed surprised when the bird stayed put. "Who *are* you?" she asked.

"Oluu."

"What?" Molly drew back. "Say that again. . . ."

"Oluu."

"But she's a dog. She ran away. I'm going to look for her tomorrow."

"Not dog—bird."

"But you can't be. I mean . . . what happened to the dog?"

Oluu couldn't explain, so she simply insisted, "Oluu bird."

"MOLLY PUT ON..."

Molly put on her bathrobe and boots, sneaked out the back door, and took the bird down to the barn. As soon as they got to the office, Oluu flew over to the *World Book, Volume B,* and tapped it with her beak. Molly opened it. She watched as Oluu flipped the pages with her claws. When she got to the article on birds, she read the whole thing—thirteen pages—in less than a minute. Molly stared. She told herself she'd better ask some questions.

Of course, Oluu couldn't answer. She tried, but all she could say was stuff Molly had already taught her: "Good night, good dog, okay, Molly." Then Molly had an idea. She leaned back in her father's heavy chair.

"If you can read, maybe you can write."

Oluu was perched on the desk. Molly handed her a pencil and opened her journal to a blank page.

• • •

The first time Oluu tried writing, the words came out in tiny script, and looked like this:

ceppppplltjtjjilbkrflfnkliflelivlekeehgegggg-ehhmtbnritjkrihjjjjjuy

Molly said, "What in the world is that?"

"Oluu write!" But Oluu'd forgotten that Molly's intelligence was limited. Maybe she understood other codes. Oluu tried the simplest one she knew:

2{ppo897^^5%%%%@~055584.39393837459 59444444===zz===+++9743)

Molly *didn't* get it. She said, "Oluu, why did you write down all those numbers?"

"Say all," Oluu chirped.

"They don't, either. Anyway, I *hate* numbers!"

"Hate?"

"It's when you don't like something. You can hate a place or a person or a thing, like numbers.

"It's the opposite of *love*," Molly went on. "*Love* is good feelings—like you loved eggs, Oluu. I warned you, but you didn't pay attention, and look what happened."

"Oluu *good* bird." Oluu looked off in the other direction. Molly felt bad that she'd said, "I told you so." She tried to be nicer: "That's true—you are a good bird. But I love dogs. Now that you're a sparrow, I have to get used to you all over again."

Oluu stretched her wings. "Bird *pretty*."

"Yes, your wings are beautiful. Let's go outside, so I can see you fly."

They went into the hayfield. Oluu rode on Molly's shoulder. Then she launched herself, flapped her wings, and flew ahead. Molly stretched her arms out from her sides and followed Oluu. Her rubber boots slapped against her feet. She ran till she was exhausted, then lay down on her back in the field. Oluu shot out of the sky and crash-landed on Molly's stomach.

"Ouch!" Molly yelped. "Why'd you do that?"

"Molly *run*."

"I can't, Oluu—I'm too tired. I have to sleep, 'cause I've got school tomorrow."

"*School?*"

"That's where I learn to read and write. Now that you're a bird, you can watch. You can't go in the building, but you can sit outside the classroom, on the windowsill. That way you can learn stuff, too."

"ON THE WALK TO THE BUS STOP..."

On the walk to the bus stop the next morning, Oluu sat on Molly's shoulder while she talked about Jack. "He was my best friend," Molly explained. "And sometimes I still like him. Other days he's an awful jerk."

"Jack *bad*?"

"No, he's not bad. . . ." Molly had to think about that. "Mostly he's *different*. He doesn't fit in, and he claims he doesn't want to, either, but he gets mad when the kids tease him. Then he's mean to me—" Molly stopped abruptly. "You better hide, 'cause there he is. . . ."

• • •

"Guess what?" Jack said when Molly got nearby. "Dad's going to work at an auction in Newport all this week. He won't get home till after midnight. I'll have the whole house to myself."

Molly had never stayed alone. She thought it might be scary. "Will you like that?" she asked.

"Oh, yeah, I'll be my own boss. I can do whatever I want."

"What about the milking?"

"Barney's coming over to help me when he's done at your place."

"Oh." Molly nodded. Maybe *she* was the babyish one, she thought suddenly. "You wouldn't want to eat supper with us?"

To her surprise, Jack hesitated. "Uhhh . . . I would, actually, only I'm supposed to stay at home, 'cause I'm in charge."

"I could ask Mom."

"Uhh . . . you don't have to or anything. I mean, I'm fine on my own."

"Tomorrow night, maybe, or Wednesday . . . My birthday's Thursday, but this year I'm only having girls."

"I don't want to come, anyhow." Jack changed his tone. "Why do you like those town kids?" he demanded.

"The girls are nice—most of them, anyway. If you'd give them a chance . . ."

"Why should I? They laugh at me. And when I do better than them in school, they get mad. It's not my fault they're stupid."

"They're not stupid! Just 'cause the rest of us don't study like you doesn't mean we're dumb!"

"Most of the class can't even do fractions. I knew that in second grade."

"So what? You're not smart at everything. If you were, you'd know how to make friends."

"I don't *need* friends," Jack said fiercely.

"Yes, you do."

"I don't. Molly, I'm leaving here soon as I can— like Guy. I'm going to Boston or New York—"

"What's there that isn't here?"

"All kinds of theories and discoveries." Jack's face flushed with excitement. "And those big cities, where the colleges and universities are, that's where people are figuring them out."

"Interesting things happen here, too," Molly said stubbornly.

"Sure—try this fertilizer instead of that one. Yesterday our only mail was about some new kind of compost! Compost! Do you know what that is?"

"Yes, of course I do." Molly scowled. From over the hill she heard the rattling of the bus. Jack heard it, too. He looked unhappy.

Mr. Collier opened the bus door, gestured for them to hurry up.

• • •

The school was nine miles away, in Glover. Molly looked out the window, but she didn't see Oluu. Could a sparrow fly that far? Maybe she wouldn't come, after all.

• • •

But she did. She arrived during social-studies class. Molly wasn't the first to see her—she was busy daydreaming about what it would be like to own an airplane, so you could travel wherever you wanted. Mrs. Lockheed noticed: "Are you with us, Molly?" she asked. About the same time, somebody else said, "Look at that bird outside the window."

Some kids turned in their seats.

"Get back to your work. You've seen a sparrow before."

"But it's cuuuuute. . . ."

"Class! Your job is to document the historical events we were discussing. . . ."

Molly looked down at her notebook, but later she sneaked a glance at the window. Oluu practically had her beak pressed against the glass. Now Mrs. Lockheed was giving them a test: "Capitol . . . citizen . . . bill of rights . . . ," she droned. Finally, it was done. Molly glanced over her paper, erased a few things, scribbled something else. She glanced at Oluu and made a mental note to tell her how wild birds behaved.

Mrs. Lockheed went to the window. When the teacher turned back, she was smiling.

"It's a song sparrow," she said. "It must have flown into the glass while we were out at morning recess and gotten stunned. We'll leave it alone, so that it can get its bearings."

"FOR JACK, THE DAY PASSED..."

For Jack, the day passed slowly. The little sparrow in the window was scarcely noticed. He won the spelling bee, but no one said, "Way to go," or "Boys rule!" He forgot his lunch and had to get the free one from the cafeteria: soggy grilled cheese and a ball of Jell-O so hard you could have bounced it on the floor. At afternoon recess, he stayed inside and worked on problems from the high-school math book. When the others came back in, he smiled at Molly, but she was talking to Donna and didn't even notice. And tonight he'd be alone. He'd thought it would be fun, but suddenly the drafty old farmhouse seemed too big for just one person. He hunched his shoulders, bent farther over his desk.

"Look," somebody said, "that bird's still there."

Jack looked. It was annoying, the way everyone was oohing and aahing over a sparrow. On the other hand, the bird *was* cute. It pressed close to the glass, like it wished it was inside. The bell rang then, and it got scared and flew away. Jack packed his books, went out, and got onto the bus.

He tried not to tease Molly—she was the only kid who cared about him, so it was stupid to be mean to her. Also, she was nice—really nice, not just pretend, like some girls. But she got on his nerves, the way she sat there daydreaming and smiling to herself, gazing out the bus window on the way home as if she were about to see a pot of gold behind a tree. Jack wanted her to smile at *him.* He sneaked up behind her and tried to tickle her. She brushed him off with one hand: "Leave me alone, Jack. I'm thinking."

"Thinking! That's a new one! Where'd you come up with that?"

But he forced himself to retreat and leave her alone.

After they got off the bus, he tried again to be friendly. He made up a song: "Molly's so jolly she should ride a trolley. . . ." She smiled, but she seemed distracted. "What are you thinking about?" Jack asked then.

"Nothing, really."

He made up another song. This time he *knew* he was being a jerk. "Nothing really is in her mind. . . . She's only kind . . . *Owwww!*"

Molly turned. "What happened?"

"Something fell on me!"

"What?"

"A stone." He picked it up and showed her. "I think it was this one."

"Stones don't fall out of thin air."

"A bird flew over first!" He pointed. There was a sparrow perched on the phone wire, like the one they'd seen at school.

"You think that bird dropped a rock on you?"

Jack felt foolish. "Something did—I've got a bump to prove it. Want to feel?"

"No, thanks." But Molly couldn't help giggling.

"'OLUU, IF YOU DO CRAZY THINGS...'"

"Oluu, if you do crazy things, people are going to notice you. Birds don't drop rocks on people, even if the people are obnoxious, like Jack."

Oluu didn't like being fussed at. Now she didn't feel like chirping, and the sunlight warming her feathers wasn't as lovely as before. Molly kept on anyway.

"You're getting into trouble, just like you did when you were a dog."

"Not," the sparrow chirped.

Molly'd figured out that Oluu *liked* arguing. "You are, too. You may know how to read, and do strange things with numbers, and even turn into different animals, but the one thing you don't know is what's good for you."

"Oluu *do.*"

"Okay, have it your way. But I'm warning you, if you don't want people to know you're different, you'll have to figure out how to blend in."

Oluu fluffed her feathers and looked the other way.

• • •

She thought she ought to send a message home. The guidelines said to send one every night. There was a lot to say: about all the creatures, and the hayfield, the sounds and atmosphere of the planet; what it was like being dog and, later, bird. She could have told about Molly, and eggs, and going to school, and being captured, and the gun. Would the Wise Ones be impressed with what she'd learned? Or would they scold her for taking foolish risks? Oluu tucked her head under her wing, thought a while. Sending the report was work, and there were many things she didn't fully understand. For the short term, she decided to beam a simple message: "Arrived safely. All systems operating."

"Message accepted," came the answer. "Currently processing . . ."

Oluu turned off her receiver for a while, in case they tried to send a critical response. She went out in the field to play. Graceful birds—Molly called them *swallows*—were darting and diving in the blue sky. Oluu tried to do it, but her wings were shorter and blunter than the others'. Then a big, fast bird with a hooked beak flew past. The swallows dove into their nests. They look like they're *afraid,* she told herself. Just in case, she hid in the tall grass until nighttime.

"MOLLY WORRIED..."

Molly worried about the secret. There was a lot Oluu hadn't caught on to, when it came to keeping a low profile. What if she'd said "good dog" to someone besides Molly? What if she'd chirped a greeting to Mrs. Lockheed, or grabbed a pencil and tried to take the social-studies test?

These questions—carefully written in the journal—led to more. Who *was* Oluu, anyway? Molly's notion that she was an extra-smart dog was blown away when Oluu turned into a bird. That had been so shocking—and so wonderful, too, since it meant she wasn't gone—that Molly hadn't even stopped to think about its significance. Now, considering the situation carefully, she reached some conclusions: *Oluu can have more than one form. Also, she communicates in a language I've never heard of.* At the end of the page, she wrote two questions: "Who are you, Oluu? Where are you from?" She decided she would ask straight-out next time she had a chance.

"BUT OLUU HAD..."

But Oluu had questions of her own.

"What is *stories*?" she asked Molly. At school, she'd listened while Mrs. Lockheed read from the Scripture titled *Sideways Stories from Wayside School*. She watched the children *laugh*. When they took spelling and math *tests,* they didn't laugh, even though the letter and number arrangements were unbelievably simple. She could remember taking tests, back home; she hadn't always paid attention, and therefore hadn't performed as well as she should have. But she couldn't recall hearing *stories.*

Molly was sitting behind the desk in the office. She liked teaching Oluu, because it made her feel smart. "Stories are made up," she explained. "They come from your *imagination.*"

"*Imagination?* Where is?" Oluu craned her feathered

neck and looked around, as if imagination were an object, like a pencil or a cup.

Molly tapped the side of her head. "Your imagination's up here. It's part of your brain."

"Brain is for *thinking*?" Molly had mentioned this before.

"Yes, but also for imagining."

"Molly tell Oluu story."

Molly was surprised. "What kind of story?"

"Like Mrs. Lockheed telled class."

"*Told* the class, Oluu. *Telled* isn't a word."

"Molly told story for Oluu, right now!"

Molly sighed. Teaching Oluu wasn't easy. But then she thought of a story Oluu might like.

"Once upon a time, there were four little rabbits. They lived with their mother in a burrow in the ground. Their names were Flopsy, Mopsy, Cottontail, and Peter. . . ."

But when Mr. McGregor chased Peter with the rake, Oluu got upset. She jumped up and down on the desktop, flapping her wings in little puffs. "No," she chirped. "Father not hurting rabbit!"

"You need to listen to the rest, Oluu. Believe me, it comes out all right."

"No. Not good story! Molly shut up!"

"Don't say *shut up,* it's rude! Where'd you hear that, anyway?"

"Molly telling it to Jack. . . ."

"Oh . . . well." Molly made a face. "It *is* rude, and you shouldn't say it."

"Oluu not liking this story!"

"You're being very bossy."

But Oluu fluffed her feathers and turned away.

• • •

When Molly tried asking Oluu *her* questions, Oluu put her off, saying, "Tomorrow."

"You ought to tell me now," Molly argued. "I've told you everything you wanted to know."

"Oluu tired."

"Promise you'll tell me soon."

"Okay."

They left the barn and went back to the house by moonlight. Oluu roosted in the bush by Molly's window. She watched as Molly pulled on her sleeping garment, got into bed, and fell asleep.

• • •

The next morning, on the way to the bus stop, Molly explained about *holidays.* She told Oluu about Christmas and Hanukkah, Fourth of July and Halloween.

"But the best one is Thursday. That's my birth-day. I'll be eleven years old."

"*Bird-day?*" Oluu fluffed her feathers.

"Not bird-day, Oluu—*birthday.* That's the day somebody's born. In this country we have a party, with cake and ice cream and presents. And people sing a special song called 'Happy Birthday.'" Molly sang it through. The second time she sang it, Oluu chirped along.

"What is *presents*?" she asked then.

"A present is a special thing that someone gives you—they can make it, or buy it, but it's just for you. It might be something you always wanted. . . ."

"What?"

"Oh, a special book, or a paint set, or even a living thing, like a pony."

"What is *year*?" Oluu asked then.

"Years are a way we measure time. A daytime and a nighttime is one day. A year has three hundred and sixty-five days."

"How many days is Molly?"

"I don't know. . . ." Molly didn't seem interested. "You'd have to multiply, I guess."

Instantly Oluu flew down and scratched a number in the dirt: 4,013.

Molly stared. "How'd you do that, Oluu?"

"Easy: *gabliee11kkkkkkkktwikk.*"

"You might be wrong."

"Oluu *not* wrong."

"Nobody can do math that fast."

"Oluu *can!*"

She flew away, because Jack was coming.

Jack was happy when Molly asked him to help her with her math. He sat beside her on the bus and showed her how to multiply: 10×365, then $+ 363$. "It's so easy when you're using tens," he tried to explain. "All you have to do is add a zero to the multiplicand."

"The what?"

"The multiplicand—that's the number that's being multiplied."

"Oh . . ." Her face went blank. "So that's the answer, right there?"

"No, we have to add the three hundred and sixty-three—see?—four thousand and thirteen."

"So she was right!"

"She who?"

"Oh!" Molly looked startled, and embarrassed. "Nobody."

"Nobody else did this problem before me?"

"Not nobody—oh, Jack, I'll explain it later, okay?"

"Okay." He was curious, but mostly he felt happy, because Molly sat beside him all the way to school.

• • •

Tuesday evening wasn't too bad. His dad had left a note and a chicken potpie for Jack to heat up in the stove. He talked himself through the procedure: "Turn the dial to four hundred; poke holes in the crust, put the pie on a cookie sheet; put it in the oven." But when Barney'd arrived to help with the milking, it was only partly cooked. Jack wasn't sure what to do, so he turned the oven off. Barney was a quiet man, quieter than Jack had hoped. But he smiled, and his voice was gentle, and he treated the cows well. When they were done, he asked: "Sure you're okay here by your lonesome? You could visit with me and Elsie, if you cared to."

"I'm fine," Jack said quickly.

"Then I'll be off. See you tomorrow, same time?"

"Yes."

• • •

As Barney's truck pulled away, Jack turned the stove back on and checked the clock. There should be fifteen minutes more . . . but when he took the potpie out, the crust was pale and flabby. He stuck his fork inside; the middle felt cold. He put it back in the oven and turned it on again.

He did his homework. Although he couldn't admit it to anyone, doing homework was one of his favorite times. He cleared off the big table in the front room, got himself a glass of water, sharpened his pencils. He opened his books and lined them up in order: social studies first, then English, then—saving the best for last—math. He answered the history questions out loud, then wrote down what he'd said. He was reading short stories from the language-arts book when he smelled something. He put it out of his mind until he finished the assignment.

The potpie! Jack ran into the kitchen and threw open the oven door. The crust was as brown as his shoe. He searched for a potholder, finally found one, pulled the potpie out. The inside was hot now, but the crust shattered like glass when he poked it. He put the whole mess on a plate and took it to the table anyway. It wasn't half as good as he'd expected. When he was done, he looked at the clock: only six-thirty. He had hours more in the house by himself. Jack shuddered. Was there someone he could call? He thought of Molly—he'd ask what the reading story was, as if he'd forgotten—but Mrs. Harkin answered the phone instead. "She's down in the barn doing her homework, Jack. Shall I get her?"

"No, that's okay."

"Would you like her to call when she comes up?" Mrs. Harkin's voice was warm. Jack wished he hadn't said he didn't want to eat with them.

"No . . . thanks anyway."

He sat down and finished his math. Afterward, he went back to the barn. The two new calves were tied to the railing; he let them loose so they could play. Then, knowing he shouldn't, he picked the little bull up and took it outside. It stared at the grass and sky as if it had landed on another planet.

Later he rubbed their heads behind the ears the way they liked and let them lick the salt off his arms and hands. He talked to them, and they stared back with big, round eyes. Then he tied them up again and went inside. The picture was broken on their old TV, but he listened to the sound. When bedtime finally rolled around, he was happy to wash up and slide between the sheets. . . .

"SO OLUU'S ANSWER HAD BEEN..."

So Oluu's answer had been right! Molly could hardly believe it! How could anyone work a math problem so fast?

She meant to ask her Wednesday morning, but instead she got up late and had to rush just to get to the bus stop on time. When she arrived at school, Oluu was already there in the window. Molly intended to wave to her at recess, but she didn't get a chance, because the girls wanted to talk about the birthday party. Molly's mom was making a chocolate sheet cake, and the girls were coming home with her on the bus and staying for supper. Now they asked what presents Molly wanted. She'd been to the store Saturday and checked things out. There was a brand of stuffed animals called Pocket Pals; Molly asked for Sam the Dog and Heather the Pony.

"Can we pat Sarge, Molly?" Rachel asked.

"Sure."

"And scratch the bull's nose?"

"Uhhh . . . we aren't allowed." Molly had done that once while Donna was in the barn, just to show off. "But we can play with Homer and Betty. She's about to have kittens."

"Oh—kittens!" The girls oohed and aahed.

"What will we do about our homework?" Sheila asked. She was the girls' star student and never missed an assignment.

"Mom says we can do it before supper."

"I hate homework," Donna sighed. Molly grinned and scooted a little closer to her friend. Sometimes, in private, they made faces about Sheila.

"Look, there's that sparrow," someone said. "Did you see it on the windowsill again this morning? It looked like it was listening to everything Mrs. Lockheed said."

• • •

Molly didn't remember much else from that recess. But later she wished she'd turned and nodded to Oluu, waved her hand secretly, or at least somehow acknowledged she was there.

Oluu found the poison by accident. She was flying around the schoolyard, landing on the windowsills and looking in on what was happening. She listened to a social-studies lesson. She learned that there were many *countries* on Earth, represented on pieces of paper called *maps*. Humans identified themselves by name and by the countries where they originated, as if they were members of distinct tribes.

Oluu was surprised at the lesson, because to her people seemed very much alike. They were either male or female, with minor variations in color, size, and shape. Thick ones were called *fat* or sometimes *strong;* smaller ones were *skinny* or *weak*. Their fur, always called *hair,* could be brown, black, gray, white, red, or yellow, but was never blue or green, unless they colored it themselves. Some wore extra lenses over their eyes, called *glasses.*

Human beings were the dominant life-form on Earth. They had built population centers—the smaller ones were *villages* or *towns,* the larger, *cities.* They had also developed intraplanetary transports that moved over land, through water, and in the air. They were an inventive species, but they were also careless.

Oluu knew about their mistakes firsthand because, as she was flying past the school bus after the lesson, her poison indicators came on. She thought at first that she might be malfunctioning, because when she went away they stopped. She flew around the bus again. They came back on. She noticed they were strongest when she flew past the spot where vapors and gases emptied from a metal tube. She flew closer. The signals grew intense, which meant the poison was very strong.

Oluu wasn't worried about herself—she could go back home, where the atmosphere was safe. But she'd be leaving Molly. Oluu knew she shouldn't care about Molly, because the guidelines said, "Do not under any circumstances form an attachment to the subject matter." Old Suni had warned against it, too, saying, "They seem similar, but they are different. . . ."

But for some reason—another shortcoming, probably—Oluu *had* formed an attachment. It had happened slowly, over time, so that she'd hardly noticed it till now. She wasn't sure what to do. Finally, she decided to look inside the workings of the bus to see what was causing the problem.

She didn't have to get close to the engine to smell the thick, sour discharge. Parts went up and down, opening and closing rhythmically. Suddenly the engine lurched. A burst of hot air grabbed Oluu's outspread wings. She flapped helplessly as she was sucked into the heat and dark.

Molly told herself the dead bird wasn't Oluu, because Oluu was way too smart to get tangled in a school-bus engine. But Jack didn't know about Oluu. "I saw the markings," he told Molly, while they were waiting for another bus to come. "It's that sparrow from the windowsill."

"It's not, either!" Molly felt a stab of fear. Maybe Jack was teasing. . . .

But he seemed sad. "I liked seeing it through the glass. It looked so excited, like it was listening to everything we said."

"It was cute, all right." Molly looked away so Jack couldn't see what she was feeling. "Why do you think it's the same one?"

"It had a little black patch over its wing."

"Maybe all song sparrows have that."

"Maybe . . . I hope so."

• • •

It was a long time before the bus arrived. Molly got home just before supper and had to hurry to finish her homework. She didn't have a chance to search for Oluu.

That night, she opened the window and looked out. There were birds chirping in the bushes. She called softly, "Oluu, Oluu," but no one came.

In that last, awful instant, Oluu had seen a *fly* perched on the road below the bus. The change had turned out well. Her vision was spectacular: She could see not just in front of her but sideways and backward, too. Her takeoff, landing, and flight speeds were impressive even to someone used to rocket technology. She couldn't speak, but her wings produced a lovely buzzing sound. And her sticky feet defied gravity.

Best of all, she could go anywhere without being noticed. She could sit on the *wall* and listen to the *farmers* who gathered at the *co-op* to talk. She could rest inside a stranger's transport, or *car,* and hear *music* coming out of holes behind the engine. Sometimes the *music* made her want to *dance.* Then she jumped and swayed on the *carpet* on the car floor.

When the driver put down the window, she flew off, into another adventure.

Slowly and surely, she was learning human speech. One of the best places for listening was the Glover Café. The main things people did at the café were *eat* and *talk*. They reminded Oluu of the cows in Molly's barn, chewing slowly, sometimes shifting in their chairs. Now and then one of them spoke: "Whather ain't too bad." "No, 'tain't," another said. They slurped brown liquid, and emptied their feed-bowls. Oluu landed on one, to see what they'd been eating, and discovered a golden lake of egg. She ate, she licked, she pranced in the lovely thick goo! She was having so much fun that she didn't notice the person sneaking up behind her. *Swish!* Something large and flat slammed down. Oluu leaped aside. She wanted to yell, *You almost hit me!* But of course, she couldn't.

When the café door opened, she flew out. She flew around town until she came to the Glover Cinema. The building was full of children, eating and yelling. It was like school, Oluu thought, only the chairs weren't wood, there were no windows, and there was no teacher. Oluu knew exactly what Mrs. Lockheed would have shouted: "Class! Pay attention!"

But she wasn't here, and the kids didn't. They threw white stuff all over the place. Oluu landed on a piece. She crawled over its rough surface, feeling it with her legs.

That's when it happened: The front of the room exploded into sound and action. Oluu leaped into the air and fled for the door, but not before she looked back over her wing. Huge, monstrous humans were walking on the wall. They were a different species from Molly, flat as windowpanes. The children screamed and shouted. Oluu wished that she could help them, but she didn't know how. She flew outside and landed, finally, on a car. She felt rattled. Had the list of dangers mentioned flat people?

By the time she got to Molly's, it was dark. The bedroom window was closed. Oluu flew to the door. Then Mother came out, carrying food for Sarge. Oluu quickly slipped inside.

Molly's house was filled with machines. Oluu landed on one that smelled like food. The surface was burning hot! She leaped off just as Mother returned and opened another. A blast of freezing-cold air pushed Oluu back and up, toward a spot where giant blades were swishing round and round. She narrowly escaped being smacked by one.

The next room was better. There were surfaces to rest on, and the artificial light was softer. A square box in one corner showed images of humans. They were flat, like the ones at the Glover Cinema, but these people were small and silent. They sat down at a flat table and pretended to eat flat food. Oluu lit on what looked like a piece of *fruit.* It had no smell, and the surface she was standing on was smooth and slippery, not like fruit at all. Just then, deep under the house, something groaned and rattled. What in the world was that?

She flew on. The next room was small. It held a chair partly filled with water, and a feed dish with a hole in the bottom. Oluu entered the hole and discovered a tunnel. While she was exploring there, someone came into the room, the tunnel entrance closed, and liquid poured into the dish. There was splashing and odd sounds. Oluu got a funny feeling about what was going to happen. She grabbed the bottom of the entranceway with her sticky feet and held on tight. When it opened, a flood of water rushed down the tube. Oluu waited to see if there was more. Then she crawled up the edge of the dish and escaped again.

The next door was Molly's. Oluu was so glad to see her that she flew up, landed on her nose, and jumped up and down. Molly was asleep. She opened her eyes for one second and brushed at Oluu with her hand. Oluu flew away, came back, and lit on Molly's hair. She hopped up and down some more. She wanted to ask about Molly's birthday, which was tomorrow, but before she got the chance, Molly turned over, grabbed the cover, and pulled it over her head.

"MOLLY WOKE UP..."

Molly woke up missing Oluu. She tried not to worry—after all, the first time Oluu got in trouble, she'd got herself out of it, too. But then she'd come back right away. . . .

All yesterday afternoon, Molly had looked for signs of Oluu's return. The problem was, she didn't know what to look for. Was she the buzzard circling above the hill? the mouse in the feedroom? the rabbit who stared silently from the edge of the meadow?

"Molly—happy birthday!"

Her folks were standing at her bedroom door, holding a small package. Molly got up quickly, took the gift, sat down on the bed, and opened it. A silver chain with a pendant—a single lavender-hued stone—winked up at her. When she held it to the light, the stone seemed to shimmer, and the colors changed, like clouds that formed and re-formed in the wind.

"Here—let me fasten it for you." Her mother's fingers touched her lightly. Then the pendant was hanging around her neck. Her dad hugged her quickly and whispered, "Happy birthday, honey. I hope it's a good one."

• • •

It was, too—better than Molly could have guessed. Jack said "happy birthday" at the bus stop, and didn't tease. Just as they were getting on the bus, Molly saw a sparrow on the phone wire she was pretty sure was Oluu. She waved, and the little bird seemed to nod at her. At school, the girls were excited about coming over. During recess and lunch, they talked about the party and the presents tucked inside their backpacks.

The bus ride home was wonderful. Molly and her friends filled up the whole back seat. They sang as the bus bounced along: "On top of spaghetti, all covered with cheese . . ." All the kids joined in. Mr. Collier wasn't smiling, but he didn't grump, either;

and when Molly and the other girls got off the bus, he asked, in his gruff old voice, "Whose birthday is it, anyway?"

"Molly's, of course. Why else would we be getting off here?" Donna grinned at him.

"Umpph . . . happy birthday, then," he said begrudgingly. When the bus door closed, the girls burst into giggles. All the way down Piney Road they kept repeating, "Umpph . . . happy birthday, then," in the grumpiest tones they could. Then they laughed and laughed. Jack walked a little way apart. When he turned down his own road, Donna called, "Bye, Jack. See you tomorrow," and to everyone's surprise he waved and called, "Have fun."

The time at Molly's was good. After-school snack was chocolate-chip cookies and milk right from the cow. "It's so creamy, it's like drinking a milkshake," Rachel said. She asked to pat the calves. Molly took the girls down to the heifer shed. The girls thought up new names for them: They called the brown-and-white one Mabel, the little one Panda, and the other two Hester and Fester. Then they went back to the house and did their homework.

Supper was macaroni and cheese with fruit salad. Molly's parents sat quietly, listening to the girls. Molly saw her dad hide a smile when Donna said she'd like to drive the tractor. "What say, after Molly opens her presents, that I hitch it up and take you girls for a hayride?"

The presents were mostly from the Wal-Mart outside town. Molly got the Pocket Pals she wanted, and a set of apple-blossom bubble bath and soap, and from Donna a metal box of colored pencils. On the card she'd written, "For your journal." Molly looked at her and smiled. The journal was secret— Donna was the only one who knew.

Besides Oluu . . . The thought hit Molly in the pit of her stomach. Where in the world was Oluu? Molly'd been so busy that she hadn't thought about her since this morning. Oluu wouldn't miss her party if she could help it. She'd wanted to see a birthday cake, with the candles burning on top. Molly felt tears come up behind her eyes. Donna saw, and whispered, "Is something wrong?"

"No—it's just . . ." Molly shook her head. Her dad got up to go outside and start the tractor. She heard him open the front door, heard him call in a strange voice, "What's this?"

"What?" her mother asked.

He didn't answer. Her mom got up to see. Molly

and the other girls went to the door and looked out, too.

The pony was a brown-and-white pinto, with a white mane and tail. She wasn't wearing a halter or a bridle. She stared at Molly and blinked one large brown eye.

"JACK'S FATHER WAS AT THE AUCTION..."

Jack's father was at the auction, so for the third straight night Jack was alone. He kept thinking about Molly's party while he made his dinner: baked beans and scrambled eggs. It came out better than the potpie, but left more dishes to be washed and put away. His homework was done too quickly. Afterward he went back to the barn. The bull calf was gone, picked up that morning by the truck that took it to the slaughterhouse. Jack tried to keep the picture from his mind. He talked to the heifers, then pulled a string to see if any of the barn cats would jump on it. But no one felt like playing, so he went back inside the house and did some math, writing simple and then more complicated equations and changing them around. He loved numbers: They were steady and reliable, the same combinations always yielding the same answers. What were they doing at the party? he wondered suddenly. What sort of cake did Molly have? "Maybe a spice cake, the kind that I don't like," he said out loud. He made up problems and timed himself, to see how quickly he could get the answers. But he went to bed feeling lonely.

At first Oluu thought that being a *pony* might be best of all. She was bigger and stronger than a dog, so that when Molly got tired Oluu could carry her. And—unlike when she'd been a *fly*—people liked her. They stroked her nose, and fed her *oats, apples,* and *carrots.* She and Molly didn't have to pretend that they weren't friends. Of course, Oluu couldn't let anyone see that she could read or speak; but that was easy. During the evening she'd snorted and nickered and whinnied. When they were alone that night, after the party, then she'd talked.

Her horse voice was deep and croaky. She'd tried to explain what had happened to her, but speaking was harder than nickering. Because she had *hooves,* she couldn't write. So she'd given Molly a condensed version of the story:

105

"Bird died. Then Oluu fly."

"You flew? How could you fly if you were dead?"

"No. Oluu *was* a fly."

"You were a fly?" Molly'd stared. "Yuck."

"Flies go everywhere."

"But they're disgusting." Molly remembered a night when a fly had come into her room and bothered her. She had swatted at it, but never come close. She asked Oluu: "Was that you?"

"Yes."

"I'm sorry—I didn't realize. You see, flies just aren't welcome in most places."

"Why not?"

"Because they carry germs."

"What is *germs*?"

Molly tried to explain. But Oluu interrupted when she got the gist of it:

"Persons *more* germy—germs inside, too."

"They are not!" But secretly Molly'd thought maybe they were. How could Oluu have known that?

• • •

Later they'd gone out. Oluu'd carried Molly up the hill and down the road to Four Corners. Twice they saw pairs of yellow-green eyes peering from the bushes, watching them. "Come out, come out," Molly called, but the little creatures never did. Their eyes would slowly back away, until they disappeared.

• • •

"I hope you're a pony for a long, long time," Molly said the next morning, before she left for school. "It's my favorite."

"No good reading—too big."

"You don't fit in the office, it's true. . . . But I could bring books to your stall."

"Big feet no turning page."

Molly kissed Oluu on her velvet nose. "We can talk about it later," she said. "I have to leave or I'll be late."

"Oluu no going school?"

"No, we really can't have a pony looking in the classroom window."

"No bus stop?"

"No, you have to stay here, in your stall. Later Dad will take you to the pasture, so you can eat grass."

Molly kissed her again, then put on her backpack and hurried down the road.

"WHEN JACK HEARD ABOUT THE PONY..."

When Jack heard about the pony, he could hardly believe it.

"Why did she come to *your* house?"

"I don't know—luck, I guess."

"But it was your birthday! You were having a party! You were already lucky!" He jammed his fists into his pockets.

"I can't explain it." Molly's face turned red. "But she's not mine, you know. Her real owners will probably find her soon. In the meantime, you should come and see her. You can even ride her, if you like."

"Yeah, maybe . . ." But Jack felt darkness settle over him like a cloud. Why didn't good things happen to him?

"THE IDEA, LIKE A TINY LIVING THING..."

The idea, like a tiny living thing that Jack could not control, seemed to burrow into his mind. It started on the school bus, when he was sitting alone in the back seat. Afterward it kept hammering at him, like a woodpecker banging on a rotten tree. It came at recess, during the science quiz, after lunch. Jack would shoo it away, but when he turned around it came right back.

He talked to his father at dinner. "Why are some people luckier than others?" he asked. But Mr. Molloy was tired from being up so late the last few nights. "Break your back working and you'll be lucky if you come out even," was all he said. After Jack finished his homework, the idea came roaring back.

There was a full moon, so it was easy to see the path across the fields. In the Harkins' barn, there was no light on.

Jack held his breath as he slipped through the big barn door. He wasn't even sure where the pony's stall was. He tiptoed through the milking barn, heard the bull snort somewhere to his left. Then—suddenly—he thought he heard the hum of voices. He flattened himself against the wall. Nothing. *I should go home now,* he whispered to himself. *That's what I said that I'd do if there was someone here.*

But he wasn't sure there was. He waited quietly, holding his breath. The low hum came again. Could it be a radio? Some of the farmers played classical music for their cows, so that they would give more milk. Jack hadn't known Mr. Harkin did that. . . .

But it didn't sound like music; it sounded like talking. Jack crept closer. The voice, he figured out, was Molly's; she was talking out loud about the games they played at school: soccer and softball and tag. *What's she doing up so late?* Jack thought. She talked more, about a story she wanted to write. She stopped then, and someone seemed to answer. The voice was so low Jack wasn't sure he actually heard it, or that it was a voice at all. Then Molly said, "Good night."

He hid behind the door. She came right past, walking straight by as if she had no idea anyone else was there. She was wearing her nightgown with a jacket over it and a pair of rubber boots, and she carried some kind of notebook in her hand. Jack stared at her shadowy, retreating form. When her footsteps had faded, and he was sure she was outside, he waited more—waited for the other person to leave. No one came. He slipped forward. Moonlight filtered through the dusty windows. He saw the pony.

She was resting in the stall, with her head down. Molly had left a book on the floor; for a moment, Jack had the strange illusion that the horse was reading it. When it heard him, it snorted, and its ears flicked forward.

"I won't hurt you," he said.

"OLUU WAS SURPRISED..."

Oluu was surprised to see Jack. Molly claimed that other children slept when it was dark.

He came up close and stared at her. He said, "I'd like to have a pony just like you."

Of course Oluu didn't answer. But she was glad that he had come. Last night had seemed long, shut in her stall; in the morning, she couldn't wait to get out and run around. She could have turned the latch and moved the metal slide-bolt with her teeth, but Molly said not to, because it would make people *suspicious.* Oluu wasn't sure what that meant, but Jack probably knew. Oluu remembered that in the classroom Jack always stuck his hand up, because he knew the answer.

Now he spoke to her. "I should go home," he said. "I should not do the thing I want to do."

Oluu wondered what that was.

"But she told me I could," Jack argued with himself. "She said, 'You can even ride her, if you like.'"

Ride who? Oluu wondered.

"But she probably meant that she would be here, too. She might have meant that I would ask, and she'd say yes. . . . She didn't think that I would come at night, like this."

Why not? Oluu wondered.

Jack came closer. Oluu had the chance to examine him. He was very different from Molly: thin and sharp instead of rounded, with orange hair and light-blue eyes. Once Molly had called him *moody.* Oluu wasn't sure what that meant.

But maybe she was going to find out. Jack got the lead rope and hitched it to Oluu's halter. He opened the stall door and led her out. Oluu wanted to ask where they were going, but she knew she couldn't. Once they got outside, though, she planted her hooves firmly in the ground.

"Come on," Jack whispered. "I want a little ride."

Oluu let him lead her to the fence and climb on.

But Jack didn't feel like Molly on her back. When she trotted, he bounced up and down—*thump thump thump.* When she started cantering, he nearly fell off. Later he figured out to lean forward and hold on to Oluu's mane. They crossed one field after another, crossed the small highway at the junction, and kept on going. Oluu felt good. There were still hours before dawn—plenty of time to turn around and go back.

"Giddyap!" Jack whispered. He crouched low now. Oluu let her guard down, and ran and ran and ran.

"JACK LOVED RIDING THE PONY..."

Jack loved riding the pony. She moved easily underneath him, and he figured out how to grip with his knees and balance over her neck while she ran. He felt as if he were flying away, into another universe, far from all his problems.

But when he saw the faint graying in the east, and didn't recognize the land around him, he realized he had gone too far.

By now he was so tired that he could barely stay awake. When they came upon a shed filled with hay in the corner of a field, he stopped. He slid off the pony, led her inside, tied her to a wooden beam. "I'll rest for an hour, and then we'll head back. They won't even know that you were gone," he promised. He curled up on the floor and slept.

When he started waking up, he couldn't remember where he was. The place where he was lying was hard and cold—not at all like his warm bed. Then it came back to him: He had taken Molly's pony and ridden it away. Why? Couldn't he have guessed it wouldn't turn out well?

He opened his eyes. It took him a minute to orient himself. Then he gasped. Where the pony should have been, there was only the leather halter, lying on the ground.

He jumped up and ran outside. He called: "Come back! Where are you? Please come back!"

But the pony didn't come back. The only sign of life was a scrawny orange cat, who emerged from behind the shed and looked at Jack with sleepy eyes.

"OLUU HADN'T PLANNED..."

Oluu hadn't planned to turn into a cat. But she wasn't sure where Jack was going, or whether it was safe to be with him. She remembered the cats back at the barn: how they appeared and disappeared silently, without being noticed. . . .

She was surprised, after she made the change, at how small she felt. She lifted each paw, set it back down, arched her back, raised and lowered her tail. The motions were fine and delicate, different from the bouncy high spirits of the dog. An insect crawled from the rotten wood beside the door. Oluu felt the urge to jump on it with her forepaws and crunch it in her mouth. She did, feeling satisfaction as the hard shell of the bug snapped; but her other, non-cat mind recoiled. Old Suni had said, "Respect life on other planets, no matter how primitive. Never destroy it arbitrarily." Oluu hadn't really intended to kill the bug. She sat staring at the broken pieces. She pushed them with her paw, hoping they would come together and start wiggling around again; but instead they lay still on the shed floor.

Then Jack began to stir. Oluu darted outside. When he came around the corner of the shed, he didn't notice her. Instead he yelled, "Come back! Come back!"

He must be calling the pony. She went and rubbed against him, to let him know he wasn't alone.

He ignored her, shouting, "Come back, please!" When nothing happened, he sat down on the ground and put his head between his hands.

"What am I going to do?" he asked himself. "The pony's disappeared. Somebody must have come into the shed and stolen it."

He wished that he could cry, but no tears came, only an awful feeling of loneliness. He remembered Mrs. Lockheed saying, gently, "Sometimes you isolate yourself, Jack." "No," he'd argued then, "the other kids don't like me." "They might, if you'd give them a chance." Now it was too late for that.

He'd wanted to be friends with Molly, but often the stupid things he did just made her mad. Now he'd lost her pony. She would hate him for the rest of his life.

His heart was pounding. To calm himself, he traced numbers in the dust. He worked a problem, trying to gain control of his feelings: 267.9 x 12.095.

The cat watched. Jack ran his fingers down its back, and it leaned into the petting. Afterward it turned, glanced at the numbers, and stepped delicately over them, placing one paw squarely beside the 0. The mark it made looked like a decimal point.

"No," he explained, as if he were a teacher. "You have to carry three. . . ." He counted the tenths and hundredths in the multiplier. "That *is* right," he corrected himself. The cat looked at him and purred. Jack rolled his eyes. "It was an accident you stepped right there," he said.

"Meeeowww." The cat almost seemed to shake its head.

"Look, you have no idea what kind of trouble I'm in. I don't have time to play with you. Get lost!" He pushed the cat away. It whirled and scratched his hand. Drops of blood appeared in a thin line over his knuckles. When he saw them, he burst into tears. The cat stalked off and sat facing the other end of the shed, as if it were pretending he didn't exist.

• • •

Later he went outside and searched for the pony. When he came back empty-handed, the cat was still there, eyeing him angrily. Jack apologized. "I'm sorry—you're just a stray who came along at the wrong time. I'm like a stray myself—I don't fit in anywhere. Math is the only thing I'm good at. . . ." He wrote an equation, hoping it would help him think. The cat turned away. It moved its paw, flicking something on the ground. Jack glanced at it, then moved closer. He gasped. There in the dust in front of the cat, neatly circled and with the decimal point correctly placed, was the answer to his problem.

"This is a bad dream—a nightmare—and any moment now I'm going to wake up," Jack said. He pinched himself so hard it made a bruise.

"It can't be true, and that's good. Just let me wake up. . . . Please, let me wake up in my own bed."

"**T**his did not happen," Jack said. "It did not happen, because you are a cat."

The cat meowed.

"Cats don't do math."

The cat meowed.

"You are a cat, and you don't know about numbers, and you didn't write that math problem, or solve it, either." The cat looked up at him and blinked its amber eyes.

Jack crossed his arms, like he was ready to argue. "I will now prove that you cannot do math," he said. He knelt, wrote an equation in the dust, stood back. The cat watched.

"Just what I thought," Jack said. "You're an animal—not dumb, but not smart, either. So I'll solve this myself, in record time."

There was something about the last three words that seemed to stir the cat, as if it couldn't bear to lose a contest or an argument. It leaped up and wrote the answer to the problem with its paw. Jack turned pale. He had to lie down on the floor to keep from fainting. He closed his eyes and took deep breaths.

. . .

When he opened his eyes again, he was still in the shed, and the cat was sitting beside him with a smug look on its face. Jack sighed. "I've tried pinching myself, and closing my eyes, and telling myself it isn't true, but I'm still here," he whispered. "And so are you. So it *is* true, on top of everything else. The pony's gone, and I'm lost in Vermont with a crazy genius cat. . . .

"Are you actually a cat? Or are you a computer toy?"

"Meeoww . . ."

"Can you talk?"

"Meeeowww."

"Come here, so I can see."

Jack picked the cat up gently. There was no question that it was real. He looked into its eyes. It blinked.

"Who are you?" Jack asked then. "Do you have a name?"

No answer.

"But you understand me—I know you do. Please tell me your name."

It waited for a minute, as if it was making a decision. Then it opened its mouth and yowled, in a high, screechy cat-voice: "Oluuuuuu."

Jack's stomach growled. He'd entered a world he hadn't imagined existed; yet the pony's halter lay on the shed floor, the sun was rising in the east, the air smelled of straw and autumn leaves, and he was hungry. "We might as well get moving," he told the cat, as if it were assumed that they would stay together. "Let's go look for the pony."

The cat shook its head.

"We have to," Jack explained. "That pony is Molly's. I've got to find it and bring it back."

Again the cat shook its head. Jack began to get a strange idea. "Maybe you know something about all this," he said.

Nod.

Jack thought about the problem. He put two and two together. "Maybe you strays are connected. . . . There was that dog, then the pony showed up out of the blue on Molly's birthday. Were you friends?"

Headshake: no.

Jack stared. "Were . . . were you . . . could you have been . . . ?"

Nod.

"You *were* the pony!" Jack gaped at the cat. "It can't be . . . but it is! You're a shape shifter! And you've come from another planet, to visit us!"

"OLUU WAS SHOCKED..."

Oluu was shocked. Molly had asked a couple of times where Oluu'd come from, but Oluu never answered, and Molly didn't seem to mind. So Oluu'd assumed that other human children wouldn't care, either. But she was wrong. In a matter of minutes, Jack had nearly figured out who she was.

Now she saw that it had been a mistake to correct the first math problem and solve the others. (*Carelessness,* the Wise Ones would have said.) But how could she have guessed two kids would be so different?

On her own planet, the young were mostly alike: cooperative, obedient, and careful. When the Wise Ones offered them advice, they loaded it into their systems and followed it. Oluu loaded it, too; but then she deliberately stored it so deep down in her files that she couldn't find it.

Old Suni once said—warmly—that there was a glitch in the technology when Oluu was created. Was she like Jack, *a stray that didn't fit anywhere*?

The idea made her so uneasy that she erased it from her memory circuits right away.

"I'm starving," Jack said. "And you'll need food and water, too."

Nod.

"So we'll go find some. As we're walking, I'll ask you more questions. Just answer yes or no—okay?"

Hesitation, as if the cat thought maybe it shouldn't.

"Don't worry—I won't tell anybody." Later Jack wondered if he should have thought harder before he made that promise.

Oluu nodded, like she was saying okay.

• • •

Later, though, while they were walking down the road (which road? Jack didn't know), he remembered something. "Last night, down in the barn, I thought I heard a conversation. Molly was talking to the pony, telling it about games and sports, only I thought she was talking to a person, and he answered back, real low." It was cold this morning. Jack stuck his hands deep into his coat pockets. "I wonder now if that was you. Maybe you *can* talk, after all."

Headshake: no.

"But I heard *something*—I remember thinking it might be a radio. Molly's voice was clear, and someone answered. I think that you *can* talk, and I think Molly knows it, too."

No.

"It's better to tell the truth," Jack said. "Don't you have true and false where you come from?"

The cat turned its head to the side, as if to say it wasn't sure.

"True is what really happened, and false is a lie—like a story, or something you made up 'cause you don't want to get into trouble. . . ."

"Meeowww." The cat seemed familiar with that idea.

"Why don't you tell me the truth?" Jack asked.

But the cat just shook its head and kept on walking.

• • •

"I want to know about your planet," Jack said, after they'd gone a mile or two. "Is it in our solar system?"

The cat looked at him like he was dumb.

"Okay, is it in our galaxy?"

Headshake: no.

"In the next one over, or the next?"

No.

Jack gave up on that and took another tack. "Are there other planets with intelligent life besides yours?"

The cat seemed to consider whether it should answer. Finally, it nodded.

"Wow—are there lots?"

Another nod.

"Double wow! And I guess they're mostly smarter than us?"

The cat nodded vigorously, as if there was no doubt.

"Are others of them here on Earth, like you?"

Nod.

"What are you doing here? Did you come because you like it better? Or are you only visiting?"

Oluu didn't know how to answer that with yes or no. Jack understood. "Are you visiting?" he repeated.

Nod.

"Are you a spy?"

The cat tilted its head, as if to say, "What's that?"

"A spy's somebody who comes to a foreign place to learn their secrets, and tell them when he gets back home. . . ."

The cat didn't answer.

"Other times, people go somewhere to learn about a place but they aren't spying—like when our class studied Lake George and went there afterward, to see it with our own eyes. We call that a field trip."

"Meeowwww." Oluu nodded.

"So you're a kid—like Molly and me? And you came to Earth on a field trip, to find out what it's like?"

Oluu nodded again.

• • •

About that time, they came to a house set back from the road behind a tangle of wild rosebushes. By then Jack had figured out how to get a meal. "We'll pretend that you're an ordinary cat," he explained. "Except we'll say you can do tricks. If they'll give us something to eat, we'll show them."

The cat seemed to think this would be fun. She practiced sitting up and rolling over and running in a circle. Then they walked up the long driveway. The house was so weather-beaten and overgrown with brambles that Jack thought it might be abandoned. He knocked on the faded blue door. After a moment, a voice called from the window: "Who's there?"

"Me and my cat."

"Who and what cat?"

An old lady stuck her head out through the window frame. Her face was saggy with wrinkles, and her white hair stuck out in curls so wild they looked as if they were ready to bounce right off her head.

"Uhhh, my name is . . . Alexander . . . and this is my cat . . . Thelma. We're on our way to join the circus. If you'll give us food, we'll show you awesome stunts."

"On your way to join the big top, eh?" The woman smiled, to show that she was joking. "I'm Mrs. Turner." She surveyed them carefully. "You look harmless enough. . . . Are you selling something?"

"No, I'm just hungry. And my cat can do cool tricks."

"You seem awfully young. . . . Shouldn't you be in school?"

"No, I hate it."

"How come?"

He hadn't meant for the conversation to go this way. "Uhhhh . . . the other kids don't like me."

"So you decided to run away. . . . I can understand that." She looked him up and down appraisingly. "Let's see just how good you two are."

Jack nodded. "We'll perform one trick," he said, turning to Oluu. "Jump up and down." She did. The old woman put her head farther out the window.

"That's incredible. I've never seen a cat jump up and down like that. What else can she do?"

"I'll show you, if you'll give us something to eat. . . ."

"Okay." She came to the front door and opened it. "Why don't you sit here on the steps."

Mrs. Turner was fast. She brought macaroni and cheese, two slabs of coconut cake, and a pint of Ben & Jerry's. "Cherry Garcia—my favorite," she said, spooning it out.

"Thank you."

Jack slurped down ice cream first, then cake, then pasta. The old lady didn't seem to mind. Oluu stuffed herself, too. Afterward she curled up on Mrs. Turner's lap.

"I don't know how many tricks this cat's going to do. I think she wants her afternoon nap."

"Uh . . . I wouldn't mind. . . ." Suddenly Jack felt exhausted. His eyes started to close.

"You can come in and lie here on the couch."

He was so tired, he hardly looked around before he fell asleep.

• • •

When he woke up, it was morning. The house was filled with light. Mrs. Turner was sitting at a long table across from the sofa, typing on a laptop. Her fingers moved faster than anything Jack had ever seen. There were six or seven other computers on the table, too, all kinds. Mrs. Turner noticed that he was awake.

"Good morning. I'll get you some breakfast."

"Oh—thanks." Jack was embarrassed. He couldn't believe he'd slept all night at a stranger's house. "We'll show you the tricks, then we'll go. . . ."

"You'll have to wake her first." Mrs. Turner pointed. Oluu was stretched out on a purple cushion in a wicker chair, snoozing away.

Mrs. Turner brought steaming-hot oatmeal with milk, and a glass of cranberry juice. Jack finished them quickly. "You have so many computers," he said.

"I'm a writer of poems and stories. To make money, I design programs for high-tech companies all over Earth."

Jack stopped himself from saying what he thought: An old person couldn't do that. Mrs. Turner seemed to read his mind. She smiled.

"I'm old all right—so old you wouldn't believe it. But I was lucky—I got special training long ago. I love number codes and combinations."

"Me too!"

"Then you should ask your teacher—if you ever go back to school, that is—to let you study some of the programs on the Net, like Com-pex. You can learn program design from them."

"I . . . I will."

"Maybe you'd better get your friend up. I'd like to see more tricks before I get back to work."

• • •

Oluu was sleepy. She meowed for food, so Mrs. Turner brought her a saucer of warm milk. Then the three of them went out front. For some reason, Jack felt a little silly. "Roll over," he told Oluu. "Run in a circle. Stand on your front paws and walk around." Mrs. Turner clapped after every trick.

"You two are just remarkable," she said. "If the circus won't take you, and you end up back here in Vermont, be sure to come and see me."

"We will." Jack didn't want to leave, but he had no choice. He headed slowly down the driveway, with Oluu tagging along behind.

"OLUU WAS HAPPY..."

Oluu was *happy.* She'd felt right at home at Mrs. Turner's. She was pretty sure that sleeping on someone's lap, then later on a soft, smooth pillow, and after that lapping warm milk from a flowered saucer must be the feeling they called *joy.* She couldn't understand why Jack wasn't feeling the same way. But he wasn't—in fact, he was *upset.* Ever since they'd left, he'd been frowning and saying words Molly'd told Oluu never to repeat, "because they're *cusses.*" Once he'd almost kicked Oluu. She'd hissed, and he'd snarled right back, saying, "I've made the most important discovery in history, but I can't tell, because everyone thinks I'm a thief. They've probably got the *sheriff* looking for me right now. And when he finds us, he'll throw me in *jail*."

"*Sheriff? Jail?*" Oluu had never heard those words.

"A sheriff is someone who enforces the laws, and our laws don't allow stealing. Taking somebody else's pony, even if you meant to bring it back, is stealing. And jail's the place they put crimin— Hey! You spoke!"

Woops! Oluu hadn't meant to think out loud.

"It *was* you, that night with Molly!"

Silence.

"No point in pretending now," he said practically. "You said *sheriff* and *jail* clear as a bell."

• • •

There was no reason not to talk to him. Maybe Jack wasn't as *nice* as Molly, but he was pretty nice, and he was also *interesting* and *smart*. He had a million ideas about how things worked, and how they ought to work instead; about what was wrong with school, Vermont, and the whole world. He wished he could be *king* ("a powerful leader that we had in olden times") so he could make things right.

"First I'd lock up all the kids who've made fun of me. They'd have to beg forgiveness on their knees.

If they didn't, I'd send them off to another planet—you could help me pick which one.

"The kids who stayed would have to learn their multiplication tables backward and forward, 'cause in my kingdom, math would rule! If you couldn't do simple problems, you wouldn't get soda or dessert."

"Even Molly?"

Jack frowned. "I'd make an exception for her, 'cause she's nice."

"Stories?"

"Oh, yeah, we'd have novels, poetry, all that. I like books, too . . . like *Charlie and the Chocolate Factory*. That's one of my favorites."

"Charlie and the . . . ?"

"That's the *name* of the story. In our world, everything has a name."

"Every stone?" Oluu batted one with her paw.

"Uhhhh . . . no . . ."

"Every cow?"

"No, they have numbers."

"Every bird?"

"Not every . . . Okay, I take it back. Every object doesn't have a name. But people do, 'cause we're the most important. After all, we run the world."

"Badly," Oluu yowled.

"Why do you say that?"

"Poisons in air, waters dirty . . ."

"Think you could do better?"

The cat nodded. "On my world, no poisons, plenty food and shelter, no fighting."

"How do you pull that off?"

She quoted Old Suni: "All is adjusted toward the common good." To her surprise, Jack didn't simply accept the idea but questioned it:

"What if people disagree on what is good?"

"*Not* people." Oluu'd thought he would know better. "People not advanced, like us."

"Aren't there any bad pe—beings?"

"No, all cooperate."

"What happens if a bad one comes?"

"It is fixed to fit. Then it is in harmony—like you say, happiness."

"How do they change it?"

Oluu wasn't exactly sure about that. She'd heard there was a method of painless readjustment, but it was hardly ever used. "No pain," she said.

"Who does it?"

"Not sure—Old Suni, maybe."

"Who's Old Suni?"

"She is leader of the Wise Ones. She knows what came before, and what comes next."

"That's pretty smart," Jack said.

• • •

Later he told Oluu his own plans. "I want to be the smartest boy in Vermont. That way I can get a scholarship to college. Once I get there, I'll learn the latest theories about math and numbers—maybe I'll even get as smart as you!"

"I will teach you," Oluu said.

"You will! That would be too cool! I mean—would you really?"

"Yes."

"I'd be the smartest boy for sure!" Jack threw his hands up in the air and did a little dance. "Let's start now," he said.

But Oluu heard something. "Car on road . . ."

Jack got scared. "We have to hide—quick, come here!"

"Oluu *not* hide."

"You have to! They might be looking for me!" Jack ducked behind the bushes along the bank. "I know that truck," he whispered. "It's Mr. Thayer, from the feed store. And look how slow he's driving. . . ."

He waited till the truck had disappeared. "He *was* searching for me," he said then. "Oluu?" He looked over his shoulder. "Where are you, Oluu?"

"OLUU WAS MAD..."

Oluu was *mad*. Did Jack think, because he was bigger, that he could tell her what to do?

She was inside a bush when she saw a little creature burrowing into the fallen leaves. The *mouse* was beautiful, with soft gray fur, a pink tail, and bright eyes. Oluu's mouth began to water. Her claws flexed. She reached out quickly, batted the mouse with one paw, then pounced. She wanted to bite down hard on the soft fur behind its neck, but before she did, she thought of the broken, lifeless bug back in the shed, and what Old Suni'd said: "Respect life. . . . Never destroy it arbitrarily." There was just one way to save the little mouse. . . .

Later she heard Jack calling. He was upset again! Oluu decided to surprise him. When he wasn't looking, she crawled up his pant leg and hid inside his pocket.

"THESE ARE SOME OF THE GOOD THINGS..."

These are some of the good things about being a mouse:

1. Hiding is easy, because you're small.

2. It's fun to climb up things and squeeze into little spaces and gnaw holes with your teeth.

3. A few crumbs or seeds can satisfy your hunger.

4. Mice have nice ears, which can lie flat or stand upright when they need to listen carefully. Their tails are one of Molly's favorite colors: pink.

"'OLUU!'..."

"**O**luu!" Jack was frantic. He'd lost the cat, who held the key to all his dreams. In the meantime, they were searching for him as if he were a common criminal. He had no plans, no place to stay, nowhere to get food. He ran farther down the road, calling Oluu, until he came to another house.

The windows told him it belonged to summer people. They were new and large—"picture windows," some called them, but his own dad said they were for doubling your oil bill, if you had money to throw away. He peeked in the side one. The house was dark, but the electric wires that ran across the yard were humming, like the power was still on. Maybe they drove up from Boston for the weekends.

"This would be a good hiding place," Jack said. "I wouldn't hurt anything, and I'd leave them all my pocket change for food. . . ." He tried the doors, but they were locked. There was a cat door in the bottom of one, but of course Jack couldn't fit through that. "What could have happened to Oluu?" he asked himself. "I've got to find her. She's going to teach me—" He stopped because he heard a click. When he tried the door again, it opened. "Come in," a high voice said.

"Who's that?"

"Oluu."

"Oluu—thank God! Is anyone else here?"

"No."

Jack stuck his head inside. A mouse was standing upright on a shelf beside a pile of hats and gloves. It waved its tiny feet in his direction.

"Jack bad. Have to say, *Sor-ree.*"

"I wasn't bad—at least, not on purpose. But I'll say *sorry* if you like."

"Yes."

Jack couldn't stop staring. Oluu was back, but in a different form! "Sorry, sorry, sorry!" he sang out.

"Not acting sorry!"

"But I am, believe me. I'll never, ever offend you again."

148

• • •

They explored. Jack had never been inside a house like this. The furniture was polished wood, with bright cushions in the corners of the chairs, and a woven blanket folded over the top of the white couch. There was a large table, with lots of candles on it; and colorful paintings on the walls and over the fireplace. The kitchen had a big black stove and refrigerator. Jack looked inside. There wasn't much: some soda and beer, ketchup and mustard. But the cupboard held canned soup, crackers, and peanut butter. Jack took them down, feeling guilty. In the meantime, Oluu was darting across the counters, squealing, "What's this? What's this?"

Jack answered her questions as he prepared his meal. "That's a coffeemaker—coffee's a hot drink grown-ups have in the morning. And that's a microwave, which is a special kind of stove. I don't know how it works, 'cause we don't have one. That thing right there is a blender—you can make milkshakes in it. You don't know what milkshakes are? They're made from ice cream, milk, and syrup—they're great! That's a dishwasher, I think, and that thing labeled Speed Queen washes clothes. Why? To get the dirt off, of course . . . Don't you wash, where you come from?"

Oluu squeaked and kept running.

"That's an electric mixer . . . a toaster oven . . . a TV set . . . a VCR. . . . That's a CD player. . . . Oh, that's a computer—looks like an old one. That's probably why they leave it here."

"EEEE?"

"Didn't you see the ones at Mrs. Turner's? They're for word processing. You can make graphs and do math, too. Sometimes there's a hookup to the Internet. Before you ask, I'll tell you." Jack was getting used to Oluu's questions. "The Internet's an information pool used all over the world. You type your question into a search engine—I'll explain that later—and it finds the data everywhere it can. Then you sort through it and figure out what parts you want to read. So if you looked up"—Jack stopped to think—"*dairy farming,* the search engine would hook you up with all the Web sites and information pools that are in its base."

"*Web site?*"

Jack explained it the best he could. "There's chatrooms, too. That's where people come together online to talk."

"Talk?"

"Type, really. The messages are electronic. Nobody can see you or hear your voice."

"Jack do it."

"Now who's being rude and bossy?"

"Jack do it *please.*"

He loved computer class, so he was happy to be asked nicely.

"Okay, I'll try."

• • •

Jack went to the Web site www.mathfreaks.com and showed Oluu how to race the computer to solve problems. Oluu won every time. "Stupid," she squeaked.

"It can't be, 'cause it's only a machine."

The mouse turned. She looked confused.

"Machines can't think or feel," Jack went on. "They're inventions that help us do the things we want."

"Machines don't making mistakes, like people."

Jack realized, suddenly, that he'd never asked Oluu what she was made of, and whether she was robotic. Maybe that's why she'd been defensive. "Humans aren't always just flesh and blood," he said. "Some people have machines inside their bodies, to control their heartbeat, or improve their hearing. . . ."

"Ah!" Oluu nodded.

"They've even made an artificial heart."

"Soon they make artificial person." Oluu seemed to know about such things. "She will be perfect and live forever."

"I don't think so," Jack argued.

"Why?"

"Because an artificial person could only do what it was programmed to. It couldn't think, or make up stories, or solve problems that hadn't been explained to it before."

"Could, too!"

"I disagree." Jack's voice was thoughtful. "Its choices would be based on what was programmed into it. Each of us humans is unique, mentally and physically. So every one of us thinks about things in a slightly different way."

"All stupid!"

Jack sighed. "You may be the rudest alien on Earth," he said.

"Oluu not!" She whipped her tail from side to side and flounced away.

"OLUU REMINDED HERSELF..."

Oluu reminded herself that Jack was only a human boy whom she wasn't supposed to worry or care about. ("Do not under any circumstances form an attachment to the subject matter.") As he got older, his processing mechanism, or *brain,* would atrophy, and his body would deteriorate and finally die. She, Oluu, could replace her parts whenever she needed to. Old Suni had said, "If you begin to malfunction, contact me at once, and I will arrange for your repair."

Jack snored softly on the couch. He'd eaten his supper, saving some crumbs for Oluu. Then he'd asked her to teach him math. But she'd put him off, saying she had other things to do, so he'd pulled the shades, lain down, and closed his eyes.

Oluu napped, too, but soon she woke up feeling energetic and curious. She climbed up the counter and turned on the toaster oven, the microwave, the blender. The blender was so noisy she turned it off again. Then she jumped on the remote and turned on the TV. The images on the screen were mostly transports: cars and trucks. Sometimes there was music, but it wasn't as nice as Molly's singing. Oluu missed Molly. When she thought about her, she felt warm and comfortable inside. Could that be the feeling they called *love*?

Later she turned on the computer and pushed the buttons for the Internet. She typed in "Extra-terrestrial" and clicked *search.* Lots of Web sites came up, but they were mostly silly stories about little green men, or human beings who were kid-napped, dragged onto rockets, and poked with metal tools. Oluu consulted her translating device for synonyms. . . . Hmmmm . . . how about *alien*? Would that be www.alien.com?

The message on the screen, disguised as a grocery list, was actually Thrombian. The sender was on the landmass called Australia, living on the underside of a sheep. A number-code sequence had been left by a group passing over Earth's atmosphere in a boomerang-type transport. Because of their strange humor, Oluu guessed the voyagers came from the western galaxies.

She kept reading. Other aliens were checking into the Web site, too. Some used coded English; but Oluu had her own decoder. "I'm going to the store to buy new shoes" actually translated into, in Kwagool, "Will depart Earth in seven mimo, arrive Waba eight mimo." "I think that it will rain tomorrow morning, and I hope it won't be cold" was Sinzoid for "Specimens from the Earthly viral colonies will be auctioned at Patrrc, Sinzoia, as soon as we return." That was the voice of a trader, or *trrrxxs.* Old Suni had given strict orders not to speak to them. They could bargain the processor right out of your unit, without your even realizing what had happened.

Oluu decided to add her own message. After all, this was her first mission, and she wanted everyone to know about it.

"Name Oluu; point of departure, 2.36p/g x 834[16.3{; broadcast point, Earth: I have taken different forms and explored this planet."

Instantly a response came from someone Oluu thought was Etronian: "What forms have you taken?"

Oluu listed them.

"What are you now?"

"I am currently a species of mammal called mouse."

"I am familiar with mouse. Is your tail pink or gray?"

"Pink."

"I love pink. On my home planet we lack pink."

"My world also does not contain pink."

"Does it contain *French fries*?"

"What are *French fries*?"

"French fries are a nourishment form consumed by humans. They originate from the plant form *potato*."

Oluu hadn't tried them, but she didn't want to sound unsophisticated. "I prefer eggs," she typed.

"That is because you have not tasted French fries. They are accompanied by a sauce in color red, called *ketchup*."

"I will look for them."

"You are ignorant of Earthly habits till you do."

"Shut up!" Oluu switched the computer off abruptly. Something was beeping in the background. Climbing back up to the counter, she discovered it was the microwave. What was it trying to say? In the meantime, the toaster oven was glowing orange. The outside was so hot she didn't even want to run past it.

"What's that?" Jack mumbled sleepily. He raised his head from the couch, looked around. "Where am I, anyway? Oh, that house . . . but what . . . ?" He stood up, hurried into the kitchen. "How did this stuff get turned on?" He fumbled with the switches, shaking his head in confusion. Then he stumbled back to bed.

"IN THE MORNING, JACK..."

In the morning, Jack woke up feeling scared. How could he have sneaked into someone else's house to spend the night? It was bad enough that people thought he'd stolen the pony. Now he could be accused of being a housebreaker. . . . He looked around. The room was in order. If he left now, would they know he'd been here?

"Oluu," he called, "we have to go."

She was curled up on the chair beside the fireplace. She didn't stir.

"Oluu, wake up." What had she been doing, to get so tired? (Did he have some vague memory, in the night, of turning something off? Or had that been a dream?) Then he noticed the computer was lit up. The screen was blank, but the Web-site address was still posted. Jack chuckled. So Oluu had been up to something, after all. . . . He clicked it off, lifted her gently into his pocket, and went out, locking the door behind him.

"Where to now?" he asked himself. He didn't even know what time it was. The sky looked early, though, and cows were mooing somewhere in the west, headed toward the barn. "Five-thirty, maybe," he whispered to himself. That was when he got the idea.

He would talk to Molly. He could let her know that Oluu was okay and find out what was going on. He would walk to the bus stop, hide, and wait for her to come.

"OLUU WAS SLEEPY..."

Oluu was sleepy. She nestled in Jack's pocket for a while, then crawled out and up his side. She climbed inside his collar and burrowed against his neck to keep herself warm. Jack stroked her back with his finger. He explained where they were going. Oluu squealed, "Molly!"

"How'd you meet her, anyway?"

"On the road home from school bus. She was my first human kid."

"You were lucky. What if you'd met somebody mean?"

"I'd running away."

They talked more. "How come Molly didn't tell someone?" Jack asked.

"She said must be *secret*." Oluu remembered the word, even though she hadn't known what it meant.

"She was probably worried about what people would do. And she was right. There's humans you can't trust—even scientists. They can hurt you really bad."

"I trust Molly," Oluu squeaked. "I *love* Molly."

"Molly is nice. She and I used to be close friends. Maybe we will be again—if she's not too mad at me, that is. . . ."

"MOLLY WAS EXHAUSTED..."

Molly was exhausted. She'd spent the last two days worrying about Oluu and Jack. The longer they were gone, the more likely it was that Jack would discover the secret. What would he do if he found out?

Other things worried Molly, too. She knew that Oluu could misbehave. What if she'd gotten mad, thrown Jack off her back, and left him somewhere in the woods? She might not know that that was wrong. She might think she was doing Molly a favor. . . .

Molly shook her head. She missed the pony. Thoughts stung at her like bees as she hurried toward the bus stop. The air was so cold it almost snapped. She dug her hands deep into her coat pockets and trudged with her head down till she reached the junction at Piney Road.

"Hey . . ."

Something poked her in the back. She spun around.

"Jack, you're here! And you're okay!"

"Yeah . . ." He stood there looking scared.

Molly felt like she was dreaming. "Where's the pony?"

"She's not really a pony. . . . I know all about her, Moll."

"About who?"

"Oluu." Jack reached carefully into his coat pocket and pulled out something small and gray. It took Molly a second to realize what it was.

"That's not her! Oluu's a pony!"

"Molly . . ."

"Take that ugly thing away!"

"What have you done?" Jack cried. "Oluu, stop!"

He chased her through the field, but near the woods she ducked under the dried leaves and disappeared.

"OLUU RAN..."

Oluu ran. She didn't know what else to do. The pain was so awful that she thought she might escape from it if she ran far enough or fast enough. But so far it wasn't working. . . .

Old Suni had forgotten one, she told herself. She had mentioned *love* and *fear* and *happiness.* Maybe she thought this—whatever it was called—was just too bad to name.

"RUNNING...RUNNING..."

Running . . . running . . . Her tiny heart was pounding. She didn't know where she was, or who she was, or why.

"They are different from us . . . ," Old Suni said.

"Do not under any circumstances form an attachment . . . ," the Wise Ones warned.

"I *love* Molly," Oluu told Jack.

"There's humans you can't trust," Jack said. "They can hurt you really bad."

• • •

Later that night, Oluu decided to return to her own planet, where there was no *hurt*. So what if they didn't have *pink,* or *singing,* or *French fries*? So what if they didn't have *love*?

PART TWO:

"OLUU ASKED THEM..."

Oluu asked them to come and get her. As she waited, she remembered things she should have done while she was on the mission, and hadn't. ("Send a message every night, stating your condition and whereabouts.") She had meant to obey the rules, of course; but she'd been busy. . . . Back home, she would be questioned about her conduct. An evaluation of the field trip would be completed, with the term *satisfactory* or *unsatisfactory performance* attached for all to know. Before, Oluu had imagined the evaluation would contain notations like *Brilliant!* and *Fabulous!* Now she wondered if it would. . . .

• • •

Old Suni didn't send a transport. Instead she answered with her own message, which arrived later that night. Oluu listened to it twice, because at first she didn't believe it: "Minimal requirements have not been met." After she was sure she'd heard it right, Oluu transmitted another message, as if the last one had never been sent: "Need transport immediately. Undesirable planet. Signed, Oluu."

The response was instantaneous: "Request denied."

"What do you mean, request denied?" Oluu shot back. "You can't leave me in this awful place!"

"Guidelines must be adhered to," came the answer.

"I meant to, but I didn't have time."

"Guidelines must be adhered to. . . ." Oluu thought for a minute that her receiver was stuck. She shot a charge of current through it, but that only ended up giving her a mild shock. The translator flashed: "Expletives are unacceptable."

"I hate you!" Oluu sent back.

"Hate is a concept foreign to our vocabulary. . . . Unable to process your message. . . ."

"Shut up!" Oluu shouted; but of course there was no reply.

"MOLLY WAS VERY SORRY..."

Molly was very sorry: not for yelling at Jack, but for what she'd said to Oluu. It was horrible, she knew. Only she'd been expecting the pony, and she'd wanted her so badly, even if it was just for a few more days. Jack was furious, because meeting Oluu was the most incredible event of his whole life. On the other hand, he felt responsible for what had happened. He felt even worse when he remembered Oluu saying: "I trust Molly. I *love* Molly."

They looked everywhere for her: in the field, the woods, all the way back to the summer people's house. They called and called, but Oluu didn't answer.

• • •

"She might come back," Molly said afterward. Her eyes were red from crying. "She always did before.

Look all around you, and, whatever you do, don't hurt anything—not a flea or a starling or a worm—because it might be Oluu."

Jack nodded. But his mind had turned to going home, and what that would be like. "What will happen to me, for taking the pony?"

"I don't know—but whatever happens, you deserve it. What you did was rotten."

Jack felt like saying, *I wasn't the one who drove Oluu away.* But he didn't, because he knew that taking the pony was bad, too. "What should I say?" he asked.

"Tell them the pony ran away, and you were too scared to come back without her."

"THAT WAS WHAT JACK DID..."

That was what Jack did. But it was hard. Everyone was mad at him, and his father was ashamed. The Harkins didn't press charges; but they told the juvenile-law officers what happened, so Jack was signed up for counseling two afternoons a week at school. He agreed to work in the Harkins' dairy barn, helping with the milking, for the next two months.

He and Molly fought. They blamed each other for Oluu's leaving: "If you hadn't screamed when you saw her . . ." "If you hadn't taken the pony in the first place . . ." But they were stuck with each other, because they were the only ones who knew.

• • •

"Now that she's gone, no one's going to believe us anyway," Jack pointed out.

"That doesn't mean she isn't coming back!"

"I didn't say that! I want to see her more than anything! She's going to teach me . . ."

"What?"

"Nothing." Jack bit his lip. Right now, being the smartest boy in Vermont didn't seem as important as just having Oluu back.

They looked for her every day—before the bus came, and in the afternoons when they got off. They talked about her, too: what she'd said about her planet, what they'd do if she returned, how they'd met her. "I thought I was dreaming," Jack said.

"I . . . I don't know what I thought. Mostly I was just amazed. Then, little by little, I began to see that she was more than just a talking animal."

"I learned some things. She's young, like us, and they sent her here on a field trip, to report back on what she found. She looked down on us because of pollution and killing, which they don't have. But I got the feeling she was having fun—like maybe her own planet was so goody-good that it was boring."

"If she is so . . . advanced, she made some dumb mistakes."

Jack nodded. "Like working that math problem in front of me."

They talked on. Slowly Molly realized that she and Jack had something in common.

"Somebody else would have gone to the TV studios, or the newspaper, and told them everything."

"I thought about that," Jack said. "The whole world would have looked and listened. But it would have been like sending a calf to the slaughterhouse. She got into enough trouble on her own. I didn't want to make it worse."

Oluu reviewed all the guidelines she could remember. She went over them point by point, as they had in class back home:

1. Tell no one. . . . Do not reveal your true identity—you do so only at the gravest risk.

2. Wait and watch.

3. The dangerous tools of each planet are catalogued. Be sure to learn them well.

4. Send a message every night, stating your condition and whereabouts.

5. Do not under any circumstances form an attachment to the subject matter.

6. Respect life on other planets, no matter how primitive. Never destroy it arbitrarily.

She had violated every single guideline. No wonder Old Suni had decided to abandon her.

Oluu felt awful. It was so hard to keep going that she thought her processor had broken. She beamed Old Suni: "Malfunctioning, must return home for new parts."

"Minimal guidelines have not been met."

"I can't meet them, because I need a tune-up. . . ."

No answer back. Oluu thought harder. If she could just get home, they'd probably let her stay. She considered begging the Wise Ones to fetch her, or stowing away on someone else's transport and asking them to drop her off. Then she realized there was another option.

What if she actually did what she was supposed to?

Was it possible Old Suni would change her mind?

"WHEN TIME PASSED..."

When time passed, and Oluu didn't return, Jack and Molly argued even more. On the bus Jack whispered, "She was happy with me—in fact, she was just plain happy. She said she loved you."

"Shut up," Molly answered. "For once in your life, why don't you just shut up?"

Mr. Collier was as grumpy as ever: "Hurry up, now, hurry up. I've heard enough of your fussing to last a lifetime."

"I thought you were moving to Florida," Molly answered, surprising herself. The old man grunted and jerked the lever that opened the school-bus door.

The air had grown colder, the first snow fallen. Under the pine trees down the road, Jack was waiting, his feet tapping a nervous rhythm. "I'm sorry

176

for what I said. Mr. Frye's trying to help me think before I say bad stuff out loud." Mr. Frye was Jack's counselor, a kind man who came to the school to talk with him while they played chess. Sometimes Molly didn't care what Mr. Frye thought.

"You could be nicer if you wanted to," she said. She added, out of the blue, "I think she's gone for good."

Jack knew what Molly meant. He let himself go quiet on the inside, the way the counselor had taught him to. That was when the idea came.

"There's this Web site that Oluu put on the computer in the summer people's house," he said.

"What about it?"

"Maybe she checks in there. . . . It could be she's supposed to, to get news or directions."

Molly sat up straight. "Could I leave a message there?"

"OLUU'D CHANGED FROM A MOUSE..."

Oluu'd changed from a mouse into a barnacle in Boston Harbor and crossed the Atlantic on the hull of a freighter. Then she turned into a gray whale and swam to Scotland, where she became a badger. She was a flea on a tiger's back in India; an antelope on the Serengeti Plain; a tortoise in the islands called Galápagos; a fleck of coral in the waters of the Great Barrier Reef. Each day, as the sun set, she sent her report.

She learned a lot. Some of it was bad. The dominant species was destroying habitats all over the planet, and fouling the seas with waste and oil. Glaciers and ice caps were melting because of pollution. Like busy insects, humans had stripped away earth and greenery from mountains and valleys. Their gathering places, *towns* and *cities,* were ringed with roads and patches of asphalt called *parking lots.* They built *factories,* where they made things: clothes and toys and furniture and *appliances* like the ones in the houses in Vermont. But many of the people who worked in the factories didn't have appliances of their own. They went home to tiny, crowded houses and thin children. Some were dying from sickness, or dirty water, or lack of food. Others fought in a ritual they called *war.* They spoke of arguments so old no one knew how or when they'd got started. "Gimme that! I had it first!" children had shouted during recess at Molly's school. The adults behaved the same way. They argued over the minerals in the land, and the oil and water underneath it. They seemed to think the planet itself was for sale, and that all the other animals who shared the Earth had price tags on them, too. . . .

Oluu sighed. She didn't want to like humans, because they were self-centered. Whatever disasters befell them, they'd brought on themselves. But she'd felt their feelings, and she knew how powerful they were: *sadness, joy, love, hurt, fear.* She wished there was a way to help people out of the mess they'd made. Maybe Old Suni could take over. She could reprogram the grown-ups, and divide things up so that there was food and shelter for everyone. Animals would have plenty of space to live, and clean water and air, and they could choose whether to be wild or tame. Oluu considered asking Old Suni if she *would* come—or if she could give instructions, so Oluu could run the planet in her place. Then she remembered something the Wise Ones said about alien life-forms: "Do not try to correct their mistakes. It is their world, and they must choose."

She tried to stay objective and not to get involved. But it was hard, because when she saw a hungry creature she thought of Molly or Jack. How awful it would be if *they* were hungry, searching through mounds of garbage to find a mouthful of food. *I have to forget them,* Oluu thought. But something inside her stirred when she remembered their voices, their smells, Molly's stories, Jack's eager-ness to learn. Then a tiny part of her answered—as if she'd been having an argument with herself— *I don't want to forget. . . .*

• • •

Oluu saw good things, too: flowers and seals and baby foxes and *sailboats* and beautifully shaped buildings called *temples* and *mosques.* On a special

180

day in the region called Nepal, women set out bowls of milk surrounded by flower petals to feed stray dogs and cats. *Kites* filled drab skies with color and movement. A mother whale sang to her baby. Human children kicked a ball back and forth. Behind a hut, bright clothes hung on a rope to dry, while all around birds sat in the trees and sang, and a little boy played music on an *instrument* he'd made himself from wood and string. The sun set over the mountains, fiery and golden, with pink clouds all around. Monkeys played a game of tag, swinging through tall trees and hooting. "Name Oluu; location 69x32/1; status: jungle parrot; condition: waiting to go home," Oluu transmitted. "Could you please send a transport?" No one answered, and after that, she didn't ask again.

"MOLLY SAID, 'I'VE BEEN CHECKING...'"

Molly said, "I've been checking every day. The message is still posted, but there's no answer."

"I guess she did go back. . . ."

"I wanted to see her one more time."

Jack frowned. "I know what you mean. But if it was the last, and you knew it was, wouldn't that be even sadder?"

Molly looked away. She felt so guilty over what she'd screamed at Oluu, that last time. Oluu had gone back to her planet thinking Molly didn't like her. . . .

Molly whispered, "I don't think I could feel worse than I do right now."

"'INTERNET CAFÉ,' THE SIGN SAID..."

"Internet Café," the sign said. It was written in four languages: English, French, Russian, and Thai. The building sat on a narrow road filled with *wanderers*. Oluu, hiding her lizard form under some cast-off sheets of cardboard, was surprised when she saw it, and that night she slithered under the stone foundation and hid behind the wall. The café stayed open late; she heard travelers chatting in many languages. The smell of hot tea filled the room. After a time the people left, and the one in charge locked the carved wooden door and went into a second room to sleep. She scurried up the leg of the flimsy table, tail twitching with excitement. It had been a long time since she'd used a computer. . . .

She found the Web site easily; www.alien.com was busy tonight. There were exchanges going on having to do with the sale of a Tituri transport docked outside Jupiter's fifth moon. The bargaining was disguised as ads for laundry soap: "Cleans better and faster, makes your bedding starry bright." Oluu scanned a series of interactions between a Thrombian and a Bactur pioneer. She surfed more pages, looking for the Etronian who'd argued with her about French fries. That was when she saw it.

The message had been posted last month, with a frame around it: "Attention Oluu." She clicked there, and the rest appeared on what looked like a piece of paper, with heart shapes around the edges:

Oluu, I'm so sorry for what I said that day at the bus stop. It was a horrible mistake. I didn't mean it—I was upset, because I'd missed you and worried about you. Oluu, can't you come back?

Please?

Love, Molly

Oluu read the message six times. Her tail flipped back and forth, and her claws dug into the table and wouldn't let go. Molly loved her after all. The things she'd said were a *mistake*. She had said them because she was *upset*. . . .

She read the message again. It said the same thing as before. But her mind wouldn't stop shouting: *Molly loves me, too!*

• • •

Later she tried to argue with herself. She had followed all the guidelines since she left Vermont. Maybe they were never returning for her, maybe she'd already made too many mistakes; but she shouldn't ruin her chances by making more. "Do not reveal your true identity," Old Suni said. It was as simple as that. But Molly had written **Please?** in dark letters and, after that, "Love." Oluu switched her tail back and forth, trying to decide what to do.

"There's something I can do to stop the sadness," Molly told Jack. "And I'm doing it tomorrow."

"What?"

"I'm cutting out the stuff about Oluu—everything in my journal, and other things I've written, too. I'll take them to the woods and bury them. It'll be like burying a person—once you do it, you know they're really gone, and they'll never be back."

Jack nodded. He remembered long ago, when his grandfather died. But then, instead of saying so, he said, "That's stupid."

"You're stupid," Molly said. "You'll keep thinking about her, and regretting what you never found out. But I'm going to make myself feel better. Maybe I'll cry—so what? Afterward the whole thing will be over."

186

"IT HAPPENED..."

It happened the next night, before Oluu had decided. She was on a long, windswept hill called a steppe, only she wasn't cold, because her thick wolf-fur protected her. She'd dug a pit in the snow to sleep in, wrapped her tail around her nose and mouth, and sent her message. "Received," came the reply, but afterward there were a series of electric pulses that she thought were random. A translation followed: "Transport arriving at drop-off point Earth time 72 hours, 11 minutes, 6 seconds. Acknowledge receipt."

"Receipt acknowledged!" Oluu sent back. "You mean you're coming to get me?"

"Transport arriving at drop-off point Earth time 72 hours, 11 minutes, 4 seconds . . ."

I'm going home! Oluu's heart seemed to lift inside

her rib cage. Soon she would breathe her own atmosphere, and see the other young, and find out how they fared. She would feel healthy and cared for. She would be part of a rational plan. She would see Old Suni and the Wise Ones and belong to the circle of contentment.

She went out on the hillside and howled with joy.

"I'M SO EXCITED..."

I'm so excited, Oluu told herself later. *Only two days till I go home.* But she wasn't as excited as she'd expected to be.

Maybe because I haven't figured out what to do about Molly. That's probably why. . . . I know I can't talk to her, but if I could just see her, and maybe leave her a message, letting her know that I'm okay, and that I care about her and Jack . . .

"Do not under any circumstances form an attachment to the subject matter."

Oh, my mistake, Oluu told herself. Still, she wasn't quite as excited as she'd expected to be. . . .

"JACK STAYED UP LATE THAT NIGHT..."

Jack stayed up late that night. He wrote down every memory of Oluu, starting with before he even knew her.

> My name is Jack Molloy, and I'm eleven, and I live near Glover, Vermont. One day in September I saw a stray dog running up the road. Molly saw it, too. . . .
>
> Then I heard she got a pony for her birthday. . . .

He wrote until it was so late that the moon had passed all the way over the barn roof and was starting to set, and the eastern sky was tinged with gray.

"I CAN'T NOT CARE..."

I *can't* not care about them, Oluu admitted. I've tried not to, and I've failed. But that doesn't mean I have to break the guidelines. I'll just look at the children once before I leave. They won't even know it's me. . . .

She was a tiny mite, clinging to the brushed wool coat of a businesswoman on an air transport called the Concorde. They would land in the city called New York in two hours. There Oluu intended to catch the first train north.

She sent her message as the sun rose outside the airplane window. The reply came back: "Received." With it was the information Oluu expected: "Transport arriving at drop-off point Earth time 28 hours, 22 minutes, 11 seconds . . ."

"JACK DIDN'T AGREE..."

Jack didn't agree with Molly's solution to feeling bad, but he did think it was a good idea to bury the information about Oluu. It would prevent anyone from finding it and questioning them. For example, what if some of Molly's friends peeked into her journal and saw Molly's questions or the codes Oluu herself had written? Would they believe her when Molly said it was only a story? And what if sometime in the future he or Molly wanted to write down what had happened? This way, everything they knew would be together, in one spot.

So he put what he'd written into a plastic bag and looped it over his arm. It banged against his leg as he ran over to the Harkins' barn that Saturday morning. Molly was in the office. "It's not that

I want to forget," Jack said. "Because I don't. But I'll go with you, anyway."

"Says who?" Secretly Molly was glad that Jack was coming. Burying the papers by herself seemed too lonely. But she didn't say that. Instead she said, "Hurry up, before we freeze to death."

She let the office door slam shut.

Oluu stood in line and bought a ticket at Grand Central Station. She pushed her hair back from her wrinkled face and spoke haltingly: "White River Junction, Vermont."

"Traveling by yourself, ma'am?"

"Yes."

"Here you go. . . . Have a good trip."

It wasn't forbidden to become human; yet the Wise Ones advised against it, on the grounds that humans were unpredictable and might contain impulses that were hard to manage. But Oluu figured she could handle it—after all, she'd struggled with her own impulsiveness. And to return home without having tried being a person seemed a shame. Still, to be on the safe side, she chose the image of an older human with calm, patient eyes.

194

Even so, it was the hardest change she'd made. Balancing her head and torso on two skinny legs was tricky; she swayed perilously back and forth, carefully stationing one foot in front before moving the one behind. Her legs and feet hurt, too, and she wasn't sure why. And the clothes! They rubbed and chafed, and when you had an itch you had to reach through them to scratch it. Oluu wanted to take them off and throw them away; but of course she couldn't let herself stand out.

Worst, though, was the human mind. It was flooded with thoughts, ideas, and feelings, piling right on top of one another. *If I don't hurry, the train will leave without me* was mixed in with *This shoe is hurting my left foot* and *Who are the rest of these people? . . . I'm hungry. . . . Am I acting like a normal human?* Oluu didn't know how to sort them out. Why couldn't she have one thought at a time? This was exhausting! But maybe other people thought so, too, because here was a sign saying *Restroom.*

Oluu went in. It turned out not to be a resting place at all, just a bunch of toilets and sinks. She went into one of the tiny stalls, closed the door, and rested anyway, leaning her head against the smooth wall. There, that was better. . . . She sighed, adjusted her shoe, pulled at the fasteners of her garments to make them looser. When she came out, she glimpsed her own reflection in the mirror. She stopped and stared. A dark, wrinkled face with friendly eyes stared back. Just then a voice came booming into the room: "Number 428, the Montrealer, departing from Gate C-3 at five-forty-five. All aboard, please!" *The train!* Oluu gasped. She limped out, followed the crowd down the moving stairway to the gate, and climbed onto the shiny silver transport.

"MOLLY AND JACK TROMPED..."

Molly and Jack tromped through light snow into the woods. Sarge came with them, wagging his tail and bouncing like a younger dog. Molly carried her backpack, with the papers inside. Jack carried a mattock and shovel. Every now and then, he set them down and threw a stick for Sarge, who ran to fetch it. After a while, they came to a clearing. Molly pointed: "There was a house here once. . . . That hole is the foundation." She brushed a thin layer of snow off the low stone wall. "Some of the kids that were born in it are buried over there." She showed Jack the graveyard. The headstones were so worn they could hardly be read.

"This is where I want to bury Oluu," Molly said.

• • •

The ground was hard. They chipped away with the mattock until they'd made a foot-deep hole, lined the bottom with flat stones, and laid the papers on top. But before Jack covered the plastic bag with dirt, he stopped and turned to Molly.

"I want to read them," he said.

"I'm trying to forget. . . ." But secretly Molly wanted to know what Jack had written, too, and so she nodded. "But when we're done, we'll bury them, and we won't talk about her anymore."

Oluu liked riding the train. Its sounds were comforting, and the rocking motion made her pleasantly sleepy. There was plenty to look at out the windows.

But the woman beside her—Oluu thought that she was also *old*—wasn't enjoying the trip. She frowned whenever Oluu scratched or burped. Once she said, sharply, "Excuse me."

"Why?"

"Some people have no manners."

"What is *manners*?"

"I hardly think I should have to explain the basics." Her voice wasn't friendly, like Molly's or Jack's.

Oluu looked at her some more. She noticed the hard look in her eyes and her turned-down mouth. "You're mean," she concluded.

"What did you say?"

"You're mean."

"I most certainly am not."

Oluu was confused. "What are you, then?"

"I'm . . . perfectly civilized—unlike some."

"Which civilization?"

"What do you mean?"

"Are you from Earth?"

"What kind of a question is that?" The woman's face became wary. Oluu was starting to feel uncomfortable herself. She tried to explain.

"It's that . . . this is primitive civilization . . . compared with some. . . ."

"What are you talking about?"

"Many serve all their inhabitants. . . . Bactur, Etronia, all galaxies west of—" She stopped suddenly and clapped her hand over her mouth.

"She told you that?" Molly asked. She was sitting on the log, holding Jack's papers in front of her.

"Yes, she claimed their society is better. The leaders make rules about what's good. If you mess up, you don't get punished, like we do. Instead you get changed, so you won't repeat your mistake."

"That might be better than going to jail," Molly said.

"Maybe—it depends on how they change you. . . ."

"You learned so much. We mostly talked about life here—what things are called and how they work."

"That was her job, to find that out. She was on a field trip to gather information."

"She was? How do you know?"

"She told me. See, right here. . . ." He pointed to a spot on the paper.

"Imagine going to another solar system! I'd be terrified."

"I'd be terrified *and* excited." Jack's nose was running, from the cold. He wiped it on his sleeve. "I've always thought there was a lot we didn't know, and I wanted to learn everything I could. But it turns out there was a whole lot more than I realized."

"Learning's okay, as long as it's not math," Molly said. "But I'd rather just imagine."

"OLUU SWITCHED SEATS..."

Oluu switched seats. Now she was sitting by a girl, who turned and looked at her. The girl had black flaps covering her ears, attached by wires to a silver-colored apparatus. Oluu heard music. She tapped her feet to the sound. The girl smiled then. "You like the Backstreet Boys?" she asked.

"Who's that?"

"They're . . . like . . . the hottest band around."

"Why don't they take some of their clothes off, if they're so hot?"

"Uhhhh . . ." The girl smiled suddenly. "You made a joke, didn't you?"

"I did?" Oluu had no idea what she was talking about. "What's your name?" she asked, to change the subject.

"Julie."

"Where are you going?"

"To Canada, to see my dad. My parents are divorced, so I go there every third weekend. . . ." The girl went on and on, talking so fast that Oluu couldn't keep up. There was something pink inside her mouth. When there was a pause, Oluu asked about it.

"You never saw bubble gum before?"

"No, I'm not from around here."

"Try it." Julie handed Oluu a small package. Oluu knew enough to take the paper off. She popped the hard pink square into her mouth.

"You have to let it sit for a minute, to soften up," Julie said. "Then you start chewing. Once you get it good and soft, you can blow bubbles, like this."

She blew one. Oluu stared, because it was so wonderful. Julie could tell she liked it. She blew an even bigger bubble, then popped it with her finger. A web of gum spread over her face. She licked off what she could. "Now you try."

"How?"

"You use your tongue to thin it, then you blow."

"I . . . I . . ." Oluu was awkward. The gum flew out and landed in her lap. Julie just laughed.

"Try again."

Oluu did. But the gum wouldn't cooperate.

"Look—watch me." Julie blew again. A perfectly formed bubble appeared from her mouth, getting bigger and bigger. Oluu's finger felt like it had come alive. Before she could stop it, it darted out and popped the bubble. "Hey," Julie said, scowling, "I didn't say you could!"

Oluu decided to move again.

"THEY PUT THE PAPERS BACK..."

They put the papers back into the bag, and the bag into the hole, and covered it with dirt. They piled stones on top, to mark the spot. "Something amazing and important is hidden here," Jack said before they left. Molly cried. "Good-bye, Oluu," she whispered. They walked home through the woods, with snow falling around them.

Vermont was colder than last time. Oluu turned into a black bear and found shelter behind a barn. It was a relief to be on four legs, and warm. That night she sent her report, and received the reply: "Transport arriving Earth time 12 hours, 9 minutes, 22 seconds." She nodded off, but her appetite tore at her like an enemy. At dawn, she went behind the house and discovered plastic containers that held bits of food, but they were small, and she had to scatter papers and cans to find them. The farmer, carrying a pail that smelled like milk back from the barn, shouted angrily. He ran into the house. Oluu drank the milk. People were yelling at her from the window, so she stood up and waved. Something whistled through the air and stung her hide! Then another sting, and another! She didn't wait to find out what it was. She took off, into the woods, and headed for Glover.

She made great time. Her powerful body crashed through whatever was in front of it, sending up a spray of snow and dirt. Her sense of direction was good. Every now and then she stopped and sniffed the air and changed her route. She ran beside the Connecticut River where it sliced through farmland and forest. The edges were spiked with ice. Once she stopped, broke the ice with her paw, and drank. Then she hurried on.

She came into the outskirts of Glover at eight-thirty—almost three hours before her transport would arrive. Molly and Jack should be on the school bus; if Oluu hurried, she could hide and see them as they got off. Hiding—that meant becoming smaller. Oluu remembered something swift and smart she'd seen in the encyclopedia. A few minutes later, a red fox trotted out of the woods, across the town green, and through the backyards of the clapboard houses. It came to a hedgerow. On the other side was the street and, beyond it, the school driveway.

The bus came right on time. Oluu watched as the children climbed off. There were some she recognized, though they wore hats and scarves and thick coats. Several jumped down the steps and started running; others flipped their lunch bags in the air. Thirty-one, thirty-two, thirty-three—that was the boy they called Henry. He tripped over his shoelace, got up, and went on. But where were Jack and Molly?

Oluu's heart beat faster. Just two children were left on the bus, two dark shapes making their way forward. The first came to the door. When she stepped out, Oluu recognized Molly's blue coat! Molly! And here, his red hair sticking up from his collar, was Jack!

"MR. COLLIER CRANKED..."

Mr. Collier cranked the door open. "Everybody off," the old man grunted. "Do you think I've got all day?"

The other kids filed out. "Hurry up, Molly. . . ." Jack waited while she blocked the aisle, looking for something. He glanced outside. On the other side of the street, beyond the hedge, something moved. Jack bent closer to the window. It was an animal, he realized—a dog, or maybe a fox. Its face was pressed close to the greenery. "Hurry up," he repeated to Molly. He pushed her gently.

"Cut it out," she said.

"Get off!" the old man yelled.

Grumbling, Molly trudged down and out. Jack plunged after her, down the bus steps. He turned to get a better look. It *was* a fox, and it was staring right at them.

"Hey!" He stepped off the sidewalk into the street. "Wait up!" He didn't see the truck racing around the bend to his left. The driver hit the brakes and tried to swerve.

"**J**ack!" Molly screamed. "Jack, wake up!"

"OLUU CHANGED INTO A..."

Oluu changed into a falcon and flew behind the ambulance. She shrieked, but her cries were drowned out by the siren. The ambulance went faster. She flew as hard as she could, so hard that she thought her wings would rip right off her body and she'd be dashed to little pieces when she fell. Finally, far ahead, the ambulance turned into the driveway of a building surrounded by grass. Oluu sank to the ground, too exhausted to think.

• • •

Later she changed into a small bird called a *wren* and flew from window to window, all the way around the building. She didn't see Jack, but there were other humans lying in beds, hooked up to tubes and wires. Was this where they fixed people who were broken?

She waited. That was the worst, because the hurt came, and the fear that her own foolishness had caused the accident. Why had she gone to see the children one last time?

She flew back to the roof and began the round of windows once again.

"MR. COLLIER DROVE MOLLY..."

Mr. Collier drove Molly to the hospital. Tears streamed down his wrinkled cheeks. The bus lurched and jolted, because it wasn't built to go that fast. Molly sat clinging to the seat.

When they got to the hospital, they were met by the school principal and Mr. Frye, Jack's counselor, and, soon after, Molly's mom.

"Oh, honey . . ." Mrs. Harkin put her arms around Molly, held her tight.

"He's alive, Mom, but he's got a fractured skull. . . ."

"How did it happen?" her mother asked. They sat down in the visitor lounge. Molly kept crying.

"I don't know—he saw something across the street, I think, and he didn't look, and then the truck came. . . ."

"How awful."

"The last thing I said to him . . . the last thing . . ."

"What is it, sweetie?"

"The last thing I said to him was mean."

"FINALLY—SOMETIME MUCH LATER..."

Finally—sometime much later—Oluu thought she saw him through a window. He was almost covered with fabric, but she recognized the pattern of freckles on his arm. The man sitting beside him must be his *father.* Oluu wished that she could sit there, too. She flapped at the glass, hoping the man would look up and tell her what was going on. But he didn't; he just sat there talking, as if he was waiting for Jack to open his eyes and answer back.

Later another person came in and poked at Jack. When he spoke, she huddled close to the window, trying to hear: "We've done everything we can. The swelling in the brain is still present. . . . If he survives, he may have serious problems. . . ."

"What can I do?" Oluu could barely hear Mr. Molloy.

"Wait with him."

"I will," the man said.

I will. Oluu settled down on the ledge.

. . .

When the sun began to set, she realized what time it was, and that she'd missed the transport.

"I SAW SOMETHING..."

I saw something. . . . *I saw something behind the hedge.*

Jack struggled to remember. He didn't know if he was awake or asleep, only that he was uncomfortable. He tried to open his eyes, but they stayed closed, as if they had a life of their own. Then sleep returned, and the memory swirled away.

"OLD SUNI CAME..."

Old Suni came to the window ledge. Oluu sensed her presence, felt it close. She felt surprised, and awed. Everyone knew Old Suni had the power to do things no one else could do, but Oluu never thought that she would come.

Then, suddenly, Oluu was afraid.

"Greetings, most powerful one," she said.

"Greetings, Earth traveler Oluu."

"I missed the pickup 'cause this boy got hurt. I didn't hurt him myself, but it might have been my fault. I couldn't leave until I knew he'd be okay," Oluu explained. "You see, I should have gone right to the spot where they were picking me up. But I made a mistake."

"Yes, you did. The Wise Ones cautioned that your

impulsiveness could lead to disaster; but you did not hear them."

"I heard," Oluu said. Her voice was very small.

"We had guidelines for the good of all. Did you follow them?"

Oluu didn't answer right away. "Sometimes," she said finally.

"We offered classes where we taught about the dangers, so they could be avoided."

"I went to some of them. . . ."

Old Suni made a soft sound, like a sigh. She said, "I bring a message from the Wise Ones."

Oluu stopped listening and stared through the window. In his bed, Jack had opened his mouth and groaned.

• • •

"That is the human child, is it not?" Old Suni asked later. "The one with whom you formed a bond?"

"There are two of them, actually. Jack's a boy and Molly's a girl." Oluu stared down at the bricks on the windowsill, because she didn't want to look at Old Suni directly.

"Do not under any circumstances form an attachment—"

"I know! I told you, I made a mistake!"

"It is understood that your intentions were good. But there were other failings. . . ."

"What else?"

"You left a trail of evidence wherever you went."

"I did? How do you know?"

"We have our agents here—like Mrs. Turner. Do you remember her?"

"The person with the bowl of warm milk?" Oluu was still for a minute, thinking. She argued, "Why was I supposed to send messages, if you knew all along what was going on?"

"We wanted to hear your point of view. Also, we were testing your readiness for other projects."

"I'm ready for them," Oluu said. "I'm more ready than ever, because I learned so much. . . ."

"You are ready to go home with me?"

"Uhhh . . ." Oluu looked in the window. "Not quite yet."

"THEY LET MOLLY INTO THE ROOM..."

They let Molly into the room just for a moment. Mr. Molloy was there, and a nurse, and both of them were listening. Molly couldn't say what she wanted to.

"Jack, can you hear me?" Her voice felt all dried up. "We've been here all day long. Mr. Collier brought me on the school bus. I was the only one, and for once he didn't yell at me. . . ." She tried to laugh, but it sounded weird, like coughing. "And he was crying, he was so upset . . . and all the girls were, too. And they want you to get well, okay? Everybody wants you to get well."

Jack didn't move. His eyes were closed. Molly didn't know whether he had heard her words at all.

Oluu stayed on the ledge that night. The Wise Ones' message, delivered by Old Suni before she left, swirled in her mind:

"While others followed the prescribed programs, you asked questions. More than once you disobeyed. Sometimes you argued against our plans and even the very principles we live by. We hoped your trip to Earth would bring added maturity; but instead, a beetle's life was lost and a human boy lies gravely ill because of you. Therefore, it is the Wise Ones' recommendation that you be rebuilt: your processor replaced and your memory banks erased. . . ."

Later snow fell, whipping into the corners and piling thick on the windowsill. Oluu tried to sweep it off, but it blew back. She fluffed up her feathers, pulled one foot inside to keep it warm. When she

224

dozed off, she felt herself picked up by the wind and hurled into the storm.

She woke surrounded by white and cold. She put out her wings, but before she could flap them the wind bashed her into something hard. She plummeted downward, struck soft snow, kept falling, until she was completely buried. *Old Suni, help me,* she thought, but maybe her transmitter didn't work in such high wind, because there wasn't any answer. She kicked and flapped till she made it to the surface. In the blinding snow, she couldn't see the side of the hospital. It was hopeless to try to fly. She stumbled forward into a hard object. She had never been so cold. Maybe I'm going to freeze, she thought. She tucked her head under her wing and waited to see what would happen.

• • •

Old Suni found her the next morning, on the loading dock beside the Dumpster. The little wren was encased in ice. Old Suni thawed her with one touch.

"The wind . . . the wind." Oluu wasn't even sure she was alive.

"It must have been . . . *frightening.*"

"It was."

"Shall we go back?"

225

"Back where?"

"Back to the windowsill."

"I can't fly yet."

"Come, then—I'll carry you."

· · ·

When she was very small, Oluu used to dream about being carried by Old Suni, held in the old one's warmth and wisdom until all her questions and protests melted away. Maybe that was what they meant when they talked in the Scripture of a "sense of order and belonging that would bring you peace." And it was wonderful, for those few moments. . . . The Earth below was white and soft and smooth, sounds were muted, no transports ran, the only things moving were the bright shapes of children, shouting and playing in the yards on the other side of the hospital fence. . . .

"How beautiful," Old Suni said.

"That snow is cold." Oluu hadn't forgotten. "I thought I was going to die," she said.

"It was a good thing I found you when I did." They were still flying, Oluu cupped in Old Suni's giant invisible wing. "You've become like them," she said.

Oluu was silent for a moment. "How could that be?" she asked.

"There have been others—like Mrs. Turner. They were never comfortable with us, though we had them from the start. Some chose to undergo reprocessing. Others preferred some form they'd taken in their travels. . . ."

Oluu was amazed, and angry. "Why didn't you tell me?"

"They are so few. . . ."

"But . . . but . . ." She wasn't sure what to say. "I was a person once."

"They *are* creative, but their brief lifespans make them choose what will give them pleasure, even when it does damage to those who come behind."

"Or those already here . . ." Oluu remembered the poison from the bus; the tiny, broken houses of the factory workers; children and grown-ups hurt or killed by war. "That's why we have that rule, *for the good of all,* isn't it?" she asked suddenly.

"Yes. Our lives may be less interesting, but we avoid the damage that bad choices bring."

"There are good choices, too. . . ."

"Yes," Old Suni said, "there are."

"JACK'S MIND FLOATED..."

Jack's mind floated like a boat on water, peacefully at times, then meeting violent winds that tipped it into the deep, dark currents. He struggled to keep from sinking. His lips tried to form the words that people use when they're in danger; but he couldn't remember what to say. Once, he thought he was awake. He didn't know where he was, but there was pain, so he retreated into the dark. Another time, he thought that he saw something small outside the window. But it wasn't his window, back home; or his bed, either. He groaned and closed his eyes.

"Why do I have to choose?" Oluu asked. "Between here and home, I mean. . . ."

"You don't. We want you to come back."

"You want to change me."

Old Suni didn't answer for a moment. "Afterward you will run more smoothly," she said. "You will feel content."

"I'm not broken!"

"Your errors put us all at risk."

"You can't turn me into someone else!"

"You will be yourself, only better."

"I want to stay the self I am right now."

Later Jack felt the fire. He was burning everywhere, especially his head. He screamed, but no sounds came out, and no one answered. He tried to slip away, as he had before; but the fire was burning him up.

"OLUU WATCHED..."

Oluu watched while they moved Jack, rushing his bed away. His father ran behind. Old Suni was silent beside her. "He might die," Oluu said. "And it will be my fault."

"I will not let him. It is against our principles to do harm on other planets."

"You're going to save him? Isn't that against the rules, too?"

"When two principles conflict, we choose the one that does more good."

"Jack's going to be all right?"

"No, he has suffered, and he will suffer more. But he will not die."

"Thank you, Old Suni. Thank you." Oluu's voice wavered. She felt the warmth of the great one receding. Emptiness began to surround her. "You're leaving? Please don't go. . . ."

"If you are coming, it must be now."

"I . . . I don't know what to do."

"You must decide."

"I can't leave—not yet!"

"Then I wish you farewell. We will effect your final transformation."

"Wait!" Already Oluu felt something slipping away, some part of who she was, and had been. "Will I remember?" she called out. Old Suni was almost gone.

"It may seem like a story, or a dream. . . ."

"Good-bye, Old Suni! I love you!"

"We do not . . ."

Oluu strained to hear. "What?" she called.

But Old Suni was too far away, or else she didn't answer.

"MOLLY COULDN'T COME TO THE HOSPITAL..."

Molly couldn't come to the hospital because of the snow. It was so deep that school was canceled. Barney couldn't make it to the barn, so she helped her dad with the morning milking. At breakfast, a call came saying Jack had worsened in the night and been moved to the Critical Care Unit. Molly went outside and shoveled new straw into the heifer pen. When she came in, her mom had made cookies and hot chocolate, but they had no taste. Molly couldn't stop thinking about Jack. Around noon, the phone rang. It was Mr. Molloy, saying that Jack had turned a corner, and was better.

"You mean he's going to be okay?"

"We can't be sure." But Mrs. Harkin's voice was almost cheerful. "Remember that, when he does wake up, he may be different. . . ."

"Different, how?"

"He may have trouble talking, or walking, or remembering."

"I don't care if he's different! I just want him to live."

"JACK DIDN'T REMEMBER..."

Jack didn't remember the darkness or the fire or the feeling that he was starting to disappear. He didn't remember the moment when the bits that had been Jack started to pull toward one another and begin a slow metallic dance, as if a magnet had drawn them from their separate lives back into cooperation, like disparate notes becoming music. He had the feeling that a giant wing had extended itself somewhere above him, spreading warmth. He swam toward it, swam toward the light it made. When he broke the surface of the water, he felt a momentary glow. Then the room went bright around him, and someone spoke in words he couldn't understand. He kept looking for the warmth, reaching for it; but it seemed to have disappeared.

"He'll be back soon," Mrs. Lockheed told the children. "His father says he's slowly getting better. But he's different, because the accident affected his brain."

"THE MORE JACK REMEMBERED..."

The more Jack remembered, the more he forgot, so that the water currents, and the fire, and the darkness, and the giant wing were pushed into the corners of his mind, and the words and faces that he used to know took over: father and dog and book and boy. But they seemed strange to him, as if he'd come from somewhere different and was seeing or hearing them for the first time. "F-F-F-Father?" he stuttered; or "M-M-M-Mrs. L-L-Lockheed?" Their faces seemed so large and—what was the word?—worried. Did he look like that himself? He stared at his image in the mirror, trying to get used to who he was.

There was so much to be learned, or relearned: walking and holding a fork and tying shoes and reading and buttoning your coat. Sometimes it all seemed overwhelming. One thing came more easily: math. For some reason, the processes—adding, subtracting, dividing, multiplying—seemed instinctive, like breathing. Mrs. Lockheed—his *teacher*—smiled. "That was always your best subject, Jack. After all you've been through, you're still ahead of us."

Jack smiled back, but he felt confused. "I know how to do it," he said, "but what's it *for*?"

The teacher seemed surprised. "It's for figuring out how many of something is needed, or how far you're traveling, or the amount of space something will take up."

"Is that important?"

"It could be. We'll talk more later. At recess, maybe." Mrs. Lockheed went back to teaching the others.

• • •

Jack remained in the classroom every recess: Getting up and down all the stairs was too hard for him right now, and the games—tag, soccer, kickball—were impossible. He stayed after school twice a week and met with his old counselor, Mr. Frye. When he could, Jack's father came to the meetings, too. They talked about ways to make Jack's life better, both while he was recovering and afterward.

238

Some of their plans involved a girl called Molly, who would carry his backpack on and off the bus, and fetch him milk from the cafeteria at lunchtime. She was one he remembered, though faintly; they had been friends. She lived on a farm next to his, and had a dog called Sarge. She was a kind girl; he liked the way her skin felt when her hand touched his.

"MOLLY TRIED TO HELP JACK REMEMBER..."

Molly tried to help Jack remember, because the past seemed like a closed door he couldn't open. "Oluu?" he asked one day, when she decided to break her own promise and bring it up. "Who's that?" He didn't recall taking the pony, or arguing at the bus stop, or saying he wanted to be the smartest boy. Instead he said whatever came into his mind, even when it was out of order or bad manners: "She's fat, isn't she?" "His nose is red!" "Look at that cloud, Molly. Isn't it pretty?"

• • •

Later he started to remember more. Some days it would seem like the floodgates had lifted, and his mind would be nothing *but* memories: playing in the barn with Molly, writing math problems at the kitchen table, the whiskery kisses his father had

240

given him when he was little. What had happened to those times? Who was he now? Little by little, these parts began to fill in, too: the kids teasing him at school, his father working hard to make ends meet, reading his schoolbooks late at night so he would know the most and be the smartest. But surely there was more? He tried to be patient, as his counselor advised, but sometimes he felt his patience wearing out.

PART THREE:

"GRANDMOTHER TOLD HER TO TAKE..."

Grandmother told her to take a walk. She pointed out the path through the woods and said that there were children who lived on the other side: a boy and a girl, with whom she might be friends. Grandmother's words were strange, like the place, which was called *Grandmother's house*. "Friends?" Luna asked.

"Others your age, to play with."

She thought that might be something good. "Play?"

"Having fun instead of doing chores."

"Names?"

"One's called Jack. The girl, I believe, is Molly— Molly Harkin. You do remember your own name, don't you, child?"

"Luna. Luna Tresseida."

"Very good. You can walk there, if you like—it's good exercise. If you don't meet them today, don't fret, because they'll be at your school."

"School?"

"The place where children go to learn and to play together."

She thought she'd heard of that, too, but she couldn't remember where or when. "Good-bye, Grandmother."

"Wait—let me fix your scarf. Are you wearing your mittens? Good! And come back on the same path, so you won't get lost."

"I won't get lost."

"Probably not, but come back the same way anyway, would you please?"

"Uhhh . . ." She wanted to argue, but she wasn't completely comfortable with Grandmother, not yet; so she nodded, even though her mind was full of reasons to say no.

"THEY HAD GOTTEN OFF THE BUS..."

They had gotten off the bus and were standing under the pine trees beside the road when the new girl came. She appeared through the woods: first just the red of her jacket; then, slowly, through the trees, a person, wearing jeans and rubber boots and a scarf and a striped wool hat. Instead of saying hi, Molly and Jack just stared. Then Molly pulled herself together. She waved. The girl approached slowly, shyly. Molly saw she had dark curly hair and brown eyes. "Who *are* you?" Jack asked.

"Luna." She had a foreign accent. When she smiled, her teeth were white and even.

"I'm Molly, and this is Jack."

"I'm Luna. I come to play."

"Where did you come from?"

"From the forest."

"But—I mean—before that. Do you live around here?"

"I live with Grandmother, at her house. I come there yesterday, from far away."

"From where?"

She named a place that Molly thought she'd heard of, maybe near Russia or Japan. Jack was interested. "What was it like, the place you left?"

"I don't remember."

"Were you in an accident, like me?"

She stared at him, forming *accident* carefully with her mouth. "What is?"

"When something bad happens that you aren't expecting."

"Not me, Luna." She kept staring at him. She looked upset. Molly pulled on Jack's sleeve to signal him, then mouthed the words, "Not now."

"Will you come to school?" she asked Luna.

"Tomorrow."

"Good! You can meet Mrs. Lockheed and the other kids. They're mostly nice. . . ."

"Not all of them," Jack said.

"Want to meet my dog? He's called Sarge."

"Sarge." The new girl seemed to be practicing. "Sarge, Molly, Jack . . ."

246

Mrs. Lockheed introduced Luna the next day. "She lives with her grandmother on Kreiner Road. She's come from a country far away, and she's learning English. Luna's hobbies are math and soccer and playing outdoors."

The kids had lots of questions. "What's your favorite thing about America?"

"Bubble gum."

"What's your unfavorite thing?"

"Stupid people." At first the kids thought Luna didn't know what she was saying, because her English wasn't very good. But she added, "You must do things different, and save this land. We will begin today." So they decided she was mean and bossy, and they ran away; but she ran after them. When Jack looked out the window, at recess, she was in the middle of a soccer game.

"Luna's good in math," he told Molly. "She's better than me."

"You'll catch up, if you keep trying."

"But I won't be like her. She's almost as fast as the computer."

"She's strange." Molly gazed out the window, watching the new girl's red coat bob up and down the playing field. "She reminds me of someone," she said then.

"'HAVE YOU EVER HEARD OF OLUU?'..."

"Have you ever heard of Oluu?" Molly had been waiting a week for this moment, when she could be alone with Luna in the cloakroom. She watched carefully, but Luna's face didn't change.

"What is it?"

"It's not a thing, it's a name."

"Whose name?"

"She was a friend of mine. She came to visit in September. But she left suddenly, and I haven't seen her since."

"You liked her?"

"Yes, she was amazing. She could do things nobody else could do."

"What?"

"She could . . . change shapes—"

Luna frowned. "Like dancing?"

"Not exactly . . . It's hard to explain." But Molly didn't even try. She felt deflated. Luna didn't have the faintest idea who Oluu was. Molly's suspicions were nothing but her own imagination running wild.

• • •

She was surprised when, a few days later on the bus, Luna made a proposal: "Saturday—tomorrow—let us go walking, you and me and Jack."

"Where?"

"In the forest. There is path my grandmother showed me."

"Okay . . ." Molly was pleased. Jack asked, "How far?" It was still hard for him to keep up.

"Close."

"Okay, I guess."

They arranged to meet at the bus stop at ten o'clock.

"THE WEEK HAD BEEN UNSEASONABLY..."

The week had been unseasonably warm, so that even though December was approaching, much of the snow had melted. The children's boots sloshed through mud and ice. Jack carried a cane to help keep his balance; Sarge ran ahead, scattering what was left of the wet snow. "This way," Luna said. Hidden behind thick shrubs was an old track Molly had never followed.

"Where does it go?" she asked Luna.

"Have patience. You will see."

• • •

They walked slowly, chatting in low voices. Overhead, chickadees hopped from branch to branch in the pine trees. The path twisted right, then left, and ended abruptly in a cluster of granite boulders.

"You go around," Luna explained. She led the way. On the other side was a small clearing in the woods.

"Why . . . it's . . . it's the foundation! Only you've come up from behind. . . . I didn't even know this path was here."

"Grandmother showed me."

"She walked this far?" Molly had heard that she was old.

"Not so far, across the fields and through the wood."

"How did she know it was here?"

Luna shrugged, as if she didn't know the answer or didn't care. Jack looked around. "I came here once," he said. "Didn't I, Molly?"

"Yes, this fall—before the accident."

"We dug a hole, didn't we?"

"Jack . . ." She tried to signal with her eyes, but he didn't catch on.

"And we buried those papers . . . about Oluu. She turned into a fox," Jack said. His eyes were wide and bright as memories flooded in, one on top of the other. "I saw her out the window of the bus. I knew it was her, 'cause she didn't run away."

"No, she never . . . Jack, you're not remembering what really happened."

"Yes, I am. There were other times, too. I wrote them down in the papers."

"What papers?" Luna asked.

"Never mind."

But Jack had forgotten the promise. "They're over there," he said.

"Where?"

"Never mind, Luna—"

Luna had already seen where Jack was pointing. She ran to the pile of rocks near the scarred old gravestones. Anyone could tell that someone had dug a hole and filled it in again. "Something's under here," she said.

"Wait!"

Luna grabbed a stick and started scrabbling before Molly could stop her. The dirt was loose—looser than it should have been, with all the cold and ice. But this last week had been warmer. . . .

"Luna, give me that!"

She'd found the plastic bag.

"That's the one," Jack said.

"I want to see!"

"It's mine!" Molly pulled it, but Luna held on, and the bag ripped. Papers scattered on the wet ground. Molly bent to gather them. What she saw . . .

"Some of these . . . Jack, look!"

Jack stared at the papers in Molly's hands. "It's printed!"

"The History of the Rudest Alien on Earth, for whomever wants to know it," Molly read out loud. "Chapters One through Four."

"Read it!" Luna said.

"But who . . . ?"

"Read it!" Jack said.

When Oluu came to Earth, she did not keep the form of her own body. Instead she landed invisible in the hayfield of a dairy farm in northern Vermont . . .

Molly read on, breathless and astounded. When she got to the chapter about herself, she stopped. "Somebody knows about me," she whispered. Jack nodded, but he wasn't as shocked. "We have to figure out who," he said.

"No one knew. . . . Nobody but you and me."

"That's what we thought. . . . But we were wrong. Somebody did know and wrote it down. Maybe they used our records to help them."

"But how could they have known the papers were here? Did you tell someone?"

"Not that I remember . . . unless it was in the hospital. . . ." Jack looked uneasy. Beside him, Luna had taken the papers from Molly and started reading on her own.

"Somebody came to visit when I was sick. She seemed to know all about me, even though I didn't know her. I don't recall exactly what we said, but she was really nice."

"What was her name?"

"It was strange—Old something . . ."

"Not Old Suni." Molly shook her head. "You wrote about her—she was head of the Wise Ones."

"It might have been a dream. But dreams can't write or print things out—you have to have a computer for that."

"Grandmother has computers," Luna said, looking up. "She has them for her work."

Jack nodded. "Lots of people do."

"Grandmother knows so much: all the countries in the world, and all the stars, and how to make chocolate pudding."

"That doesn't mean she knows things about *me*, Luna, or Molly either."

"She might," Luna said stubbornly.

"Have it your way. . . ." Jack sighed. Sometimes

Luna was such a know-it-all. And now Molly was asking:

"What are we going to do with the story? Should we bury it again?"

"I guess. But first let's finish reading it."

Molly straightened the pages. "We can do it now."

• • •

Afterward they wrapped the papers in the plastic bag and set it in the hole. They filled the hole with dirt, stomped it flat, and set the stones back on top.

"Next time we come there will be more of it," Jack said. "We can see what happens next."

"But we know . . ." Molly didn't finish the sentence because Luna was there. Luna noticed, but she didn't seem to mind.

"I've heard that story before," she said.

"You couldn't have!"

"I could too!"

"Then tell us what happens."

"Uhhh . . . I don't remember." Suddenly Luna's eyes filled with tears. Molly was surprised. She reached over and took her hand.

"It doesn't matter," she said.

Just then a bright red bird flew into the clearing and landed on the low stone wall. Another one came, too, duller than the first but still so beautiful that Luna gasped. Jack remembered what they were called.

"Cardinals . . ."

Molly smiled at him. He reached over and took her other hand, and she didn't pull it away.

"GRANDMOTHER PULLED HER PADDED ROCKING CHAIR..."

Grandmother pulled her padded rocking chair up close, as she did every night after she tucked Luna into bed. "Once upon a time," she said, "there was a girl, and her name was—"

"Oluu," Luna said.

"Oluu?" Grandmother looked surprised.

Luna nodded. "She was a friend of Molly and Jack's."

Grandmother sipped her cup of tea and rocked for a moment as she often did before saying more. "There was a girl named Oluu, and she came from far away, and she had a little brother named Michael."

"She didn't," Luna said. "They would have said so."

"They might not have."

"They would too! And the story doesn't say—"

"Luna, why must you argue so?" Grandmother frowned.

"Because I'm right. . . ."

"Oh, my. If you know all about this girl—this *Oluu*—why don't *you* tell the story?"

"Because I don't know *enough*." Luna sat up in bed. "But she was special," she said. "More special than me."

"That's hard to believe."

"Not for Mrs. Lockheed. She says I am at times . . . bossy, and lacking self-control."

Grandmother sighed. "Perhaps she said that in a moment of pique."

"She said it when I broke William's Lego rocket."

"Luna, why did you do that?"

"Because he's bad." Luna shifted uncomfortably, then peered at her elbow as if there might be something wrong with it.

"Why did you break the rocket?" Grandmother's voice was patient.

"He called me weirdo, because I can run faster than him. And he said my name is strange."

"You mustn't harm people or their possessions. Can you promise that you won't?"

"No."

"Why not?"

"Because I like breaking things sometimes." She thought for a moment. "Especially if they're William's."

"If you do it again, I'll have to punish you."

"He shouldn't say I'm strange."

"No, he shouldn't, but we can't control *his* behavior. Anyway, I like your name." Grandmother said it aloud. "It sounds joyful."

"But we should be called the same, you and me—like Harkins or Johnsons or Molloys."

"I enjoy having my own name, different from anyone else's."

"Your mother and father had that last name."

"I don't remember them," Grandmother said.

"Because you left when you were young?"

"That's right."

"And you lived here by yourself?"

Grandmother nodded.

"Until I came. . . ."

"Until you came."

Luna looked right into her grandmother's face. "We're not like Molly and Jack, are we?"

"We are like them, except that we'll live longer,

and we're extra smart. There are a few other differences, but they don't notice, not really. They are individuals, so they expect variety, and their world has room for all kinds of thinking and imagining. People may argue with you, but they can't take your ideas away, even if your thoughts are silly or mean or don't make sense. That's one reason I came here."

"Not me." Luna said that mostly just to disagree. She lay back against her pillow, looking thoughtful. "There is a name for dogs and cats who wander . . ."

"We're not strays, Luna. We have a home, and we have each other."

"You don't want somebody . . . better?"

"I opened the door to all who came," Grandmother said. "But you were the one . . . "

Then, instead of simply remembering, Luna felt: *a sudden impact, her sensors opening to the cold and dark. She was afraid. She didn't know where she was, or who, or why. There were stars above her, but they weren't the ones she was used to. Her form was different, too: it was awkward, with four oddly shaped limbs, and a trunk with a furry ovoid on top. She had some memory of it: from the classes, maybe? Was it one that moved on just two limbs?*

While she was thinking, the body began to shake. She used the shorter limbs to push herself upright. Plant forms, squat and thick, surrounded her. She found a woven garment on the ground and pulled it close, but the trembling continued. She moved forward, to the side. The plants pulled at her with their wiry grippers. Cold crystals crunched beneath her. A light shone up ahead, too close to the horizon to be a star. As she came near, she saw there was a shelter. She stood in front of it, unsure of what to do. But warmth seeped through the edges of the entrance hole, so she pushed against it. It didn't budge. She pushed again, then smacked it with one limb—once, twice, three times. She was about to turn away when suddenly it opened a tiny bit.

"Who's there?"

"Luna. Luna Tresseida." She wasn't sure where the words came from, or how she knew to utter them.

It opened wider. In the space behind were light and warmth, but blocking them was a creature much like herself.

"Luna?" She repeated the name.

"Luna Tresseida. I . . . I have arrived."

The other spread her limbs out wide. "I am Hana
Galta Turner, and I've been waiting for you." She
embraced her. Luna felt different . . . wonderful. She
had never dreamed that she could feel that good.

"It's been so long," the other one said. "And,
finally, you've come home. Sit by the stove and
warm yourself, and I'll fetch a bowl of soup. . . ."

• • •

Grandmother rose from the rocking chair to kiss
Luna good night. But Luna's eyes flew open and
she hugged her grandmother as tightly as she
could. "I wasn't asleep," she said. "I was remembering the day I came."

"Oh."

"And why I came. It wasn't just about having my
own ideas. There was something I wanted to say."

"What?"

"I love you." Luna paused. Her voice sounded
thinner, more fragile, than usual. "I love you,
Grandmother."

Grandmother smiled a smile that seemed to
come from everywhere. "I love you, too." She kissed
the little girl and pulled the covers up, as if she
were about to go.

"But the story!" Luna cried. "You didn't tell the story!"

"Oh my." The old woman sat back down. She rocked and thought and rocked. When she spoke her voice was soft and low. "Once upon a time, there was a girl, and her name . . ."